JENNIFER S. ALDERSON

Collecting Can Be Murder

First published by Traveling Life Press 2023

First edition

ISBN: 9789083169743

This book was professionally typeset on Reedsy.
Find out more at reedsy.com

Contents

1

Wakey Wakey

"Carmen—wake up!" A light slap greeted my return to consciousness. All around me, voices were crying out, gasping in fear or surprise; I couldn't tell for certain which. But their anxiety was audible.

I opened my eyes and saw a fuzzy version of the Baroness, my favorite partner in crime, hovering over me.

When she raised her hand to strike my cheek again, I caught it midswing. "I'm awake."

"Talk to me! Who are you?" Lady Sophie Rutherford—or the Baroness, as I called her—knelt down, the hem of her aquamarine ball gown spreading out around her like a silky pool of water, and grabbed hold of my shoulders, shaking me as hard as her social status allowed.

"Carmen De Luca, art sleuth," I mumbled as I ran my fingers over my temple, wincing when I hit broken skin. "Why is there a baseball growing out of my forehead?"

"It looks like you got hit by a whole lot of books. Those covers aren't soft at all. Or maybe the bookshelf nicked you."

"The bookcase!" My last memory before I lost consciousness was of a mass of books racing towards me. I sat up far too quickly, jarring my bruised skull. Several hardcovers slid off of my chest, adding tiny bruises to my list of injuries. I squeezed my eyes shut and lay back down.

"I guess it did hit me. How's Harold?"

The Baroness's eyes widened slightly, enough to tell me something was very wrong. "He took the brunt of it."

My brain screamed for me to remain still, but I had to see what had happened to my target. I pushed myself up onto my elbows and followed my partner's gaze over to the ceiling-high bookcase that had been filled with hundreds of rare first editions when I had entered. It was now lying across the room, its valuable contents strewn over the floor and furniture.

The legs of the chair that had been closest to the bookcase had been crushed by the heavy planks, as if they were toothpicks. Sticking out from under the shelving were a pair of burgundy pants and alligator-skin boots—the same ensemble our party's flamboyant host, Harold Moreau, had been wearing this evening.

Neither the legs nor boots were moving. Billy, a curator at a literature museum on the East Coast, and two of the collectors invited to the private viewing were busy clearing the many books covering Harold's body, chucking the pricey volumes behind them in their rush to reach his face.

Several almost nicked Harold's wife, Tammy, who was pacing the floor, seemingly unaware of the heavy books being thrown in her direction.

"I told Harold that bookshelf was top-heavy, but he wouldn't listen. Instead, he kept buying more and more. It wasn't a hobby anymore, it was an illness. No wonder it toppled over!"

"That's not right. I saw a pair of arms pushing the bookcase, just before everything went black," I muttered, too softly for the anxious wife to hear.

The Baroness leaned in close to my ear. "Are you sure? That would mean..."

"That someone intentionally pushed it onto Harold. He was sitting in that chair when it fell." I groaned when a horrible thought struck. "He wouldn't have been able to react and perhaps save himself, either, thanks to the chloroform I'd administered. But why would someone want to harm him?"

I studied the scene before me. The books that had tumbled from the fallen bookshelf littered the floor in piles several volumes deep. Our host had boasted that the case held his most prized first editions. They weren't as valuable as his multimillion-dollar collection of medieval prayer books, but were still worth a pretty penny and far easier to sell off than the ancient volumes. If someone had intended to disarm Harold so they could steal them, they had botched the job.

So if that wasn't their goal, what was?

When I took another gander around the space, something else sent chills up my spine. Several of the books of hours that had been displayed in the glass cases lining the back wall when I entered were no longer there. I scanned the volumes scattered all around me, but didn't see any of the illuminated manuscripts' gold- and silver-lined covers shining back at me.

"Baroness, several of Harold's prayer books appear to be missing." When I jiggled my head towards the closest display case, it felt like someone was taking a hammer to my skull.

My partner grabbed my arm, her nails digging into my skin. "Where is the Avron book?"

"In my purse."

"Why is it in your purse?" The Baroness's voice rose an octave as her face paled considerably. "You weren't authorized to take it."

I tuned her voice out as I reached for my bag, luckily still by my side, expecting to feel a hard lump where the illuminated manuscript should have been. All I felt was overpriced leather and my hairbrush. I rubbed gingerly at my forehead, trying to recall my exact movements, until those final moments before I lost consciousness replayed in my mind. Of course the book wasn't in my purse—I had been preparing it for transport when the bookcase came crashing down on me.

"Baroness, we have a problem. Mission not accomplished."

She nodded towards Harold. "We have more than one, by the looks of things."

The three men were still busy removing the mountain of books smothering our host, their tempo bordering on frantic as Harold's face finally came into view.

"Harold! Can you hear me?" Billy screamed.

"I've got a bad feeling about this," I whispered to my partner. She squeezed my hand tight as we watched the others tend to our party's host.

When Harold's face was clear, one of the guests shoved a mirror under his nose, while another searched for a pulse.

"How is he doing?" I dared to ask.

Billy leaned back on his haunches and shook his head. "Not as lucky as you, I'm afraid. Harold is dead."

2

Other Priorities

"This is Tammy Moreau of Villa Saint Marie. My husband, Harold, is dead!" our hostess cried into the phone. Her high-pitched voice was choked with tears, making her words almost incomprehensible.

We had moved to the other side of the library, leaving our host's body still partially buried under a pile of hardbacks. Billy had closed the doors so that the noise from the party taking place across the hall would not disturb Tammy's conversation.

I was as shocked that our host was gone as I was that a French policeman spoke English out here in the boondocks. We were a good hour away from any sort of metropolis, in a tiny village on the coast of Brittany where the cows and sheep vastly outnumbered the humans. The Moreaus may have had French roots on Harold's paternal side, but both he and Tammy were American through and through. It was only because the eccentric millionaire decided to buy this expansive villa last year that they were now situated in Europe.

Their new home was one of several built by Swiss architect Le Corbusier, a modernist credited with fathering the Bauhaus movement. "House" was not the correct term for something so spacious; rather, "villa" or "mansion" would've been a more accurate description of this monumental structure. Apparently the architect agreed, for the house had been given a name—Villa Saint Marie.

There were three stories of elevated living space, as well as a tiny garden on the roof. To reach the front door, guests had to circumvent a forest of concrete columns that supported the upper floors. The sparse modernism of the structure contrasted greatly with our hostess's choice of furnishings. Tammy clearly preferred a more romantic style of furniture—vintage pieces made from ornamental, curvy dark wood and decorated with carvings, pearl inlays, and plush fabrics. The paintings and carpets covering the concrete walls were a mishmash of medieval-looking tapestries, floral still lifes, and pastoral landscapes.

During the party, our hostess had shared her passion for shopping at *les brocanteurs*, or the local antique shops. As I eyed the eighteenth-century reading table we were gathered around, its walnut sides and legs decorated with the carved heads of lions and knights, it was obvious that she had spared no expense. This piece alone cost upwards of a hundred thousand dollars, and the high-back chairs we were sitting in were another grand apiece.

Thanks to her choices, it was almost as if our hostess was turning her nose up at Le Corbusier's modernistic vision on home design. Before I could contemplate what sort of furnishings I would have filled this home with, Tammy spoke up again.

"Of course, I am certain. There's no pulse, and he's not breathing. Harold is gone."

As the lady of the villa listened to the police's response, her heavily botoxed forehead crinkled ever so slightly. "How can my Harold not be a priority? I don't care if electricity poles are trapping people in their cars—my husband is dead, and I expect you to do something about it!"

Her eyes narrowed to slits as she listened once again. Tammy was clearly a woman used to getting what she wanted, but I had a feeling things weren't working out as she'd expected this time.

"Fine. It sounds as if we have no choice." Her curt farewell, punctuated by a flick of the wrist as she dropped the receiver into the cradle, thereby hanging up on the local chief of police, confirmed my suspicions.

She pinched the bridge of her nose ever so slightly before looking up at the small crowd seated around the reading table. Across from me and the

Baroness sat Billy the curator and the pair of collectors who had helped to pull books off of Harold's body.

Tammy's squeaky voice disrupted my thoughts once again. "Well, that's that. The police aren't going to do anything about Harold, at least not tonight. The storm has maxed out their resources and they have to put emergencies before corpses."

She sighed deeply as she stared off towards her husband's body, lying a few feet away. "I'm afraid my Harold is going to have to stay where he's at for a few more hours. At least he passed away in his favorite room."

I cocked my head slightly as I studied the newly widowed woman. Other than her initial tears, she didn't seem overly distraught by her husband's death—more put out that she had to deal with the consequences. Having been raised by a single mother who never had time to date, I didn't really know what constituted a happy relationship, but I had expected more tears.

"I better inform the other guests," Tammy said as she grabbed her handbag from one of the chairs. The ringing doorbell caused her lips to purse even further. "Who could that be?"

Billy's face brightened up. "Maybe the police did send someone over!"

When Tammy started walking towards the entrance, I followed as quickly as my head allowed, curious to see who had braved the storm. The rest must have had the same idea, because they were right behind me.

We were halfway across the black-and-white tiled entrance hall when the butler opened the door, letting in a sheet of rain. Lightning tore across the sky, lighting up the figure standing in the threshold.

"Mother!" A young man, not much older than thirty and drenched to the skin, rushed up the stairs to Tammy. "Sorry that I'm so late."

He leaned in to kiss his mother's cheek, but she pulled back and grabbed his hands, instead. "Roger—I'm just glad you made it in one piece! But sweetheart, I have terrible news. Your father is dead."

"What?" Roger fell back against the wall, his woolen overcoat soaking a medieval tapestry. "Where is he?"

"With his books, but I don't think you should see him like th—"

Tammy didn't get the chance to finish her sentence because Roger was already racing towards the library. I tore after him—as did the rest—curious to see how he would react to his father's tragic demise. As expected, the young man was downright inconsolable.

He held onto his father's foot as sobs racked his body. When his tears subsided, Roger tugged on the heavy bookcase. "We can't leave him like this. Help me get this thing off of him."

He shed his wet jacket and reached for one corner of the bookcase. When he did, one of his golden cufflinks briefly caught the light. The men in the room silently joined in, all pulling on the heavy wooden planks, trying to right it. Seeing as I was probably stronger than the most of them, I could have helped, but it wasn't worth blowing my cover as a meek, yet brainy, antiques journalist to do so. Besides, it wouldn't have mattered because the books that had fallen off of the lower shelves were blocking the base of the case and preventing the men from setting it back up.

"We'll have to move more of the books out of the way of its feet first," Billy, the curator, reasoned. He bent over and grabbed a stack of first editions. As he rose, his high-pitched voice echoed through the space. "Tammy—you have to see this!"

"What is there?"

"The bolt holding the bookcase to the floor has been removed!"

"How could that be? Harold had propped so many books into it, I was worried it would fall over. But he assured me the four bolts would hold it in place. He pointed them out to me only a week ago."

Tammy stared down at the large bracket, its screw hole empty. "I don't see any sign of this one. If it had snapped off, part of it should still be stuck in the wood. Without those bolts in place, a child could have pushed the bookcase over."

Her cheeks drained of color as her hand flew to her chest. "My Harold was murdered!"

She turned an accusatory eye towards me.

"What are you looking at me for? The bookshelf hit me, too, which means I couldn't have pushed it over. And why would I harm him—I was going to feature his collection in my magazine and we hadn't finished our interview yet." It sounded callous, I knew, but I was there as a reporter. Getting emotional about his death would have been out of character.

Roger stood before the group and held out his hands, as if warding us away. "If someone killed Dad, then that makes this a crime scene. I say we all stay out of the library until the police arrive."

His mother wrapped an arm around him and shivered. "I agree. Let's get back to the party. There is safety in numbers."

"What's that supposed to mean?" I whispered to the Baroness.

"I'm assuming it's the jet lag and head wound that are making you slow. My dear partner, if Harold was murdered, then someone at this party killed him."

3

Killer Party

"Carmen, darling, I know you are a consummate professional and I trust your judgment completely. Yet, I do wonder why you felt compelled to take the Avron manuscript," the Baroness whispered as she took my elbow and propelled me back towards the living room, where the party was still in full swing. The jazz music had been replaced by electronic house, its deep bass vibrating the wooden floorboards and my injured brain.

I gazed down at my partner, puzzled by her question. "Harold was adamant that he would never part with any of his illuminated manuscripts, now that he had the largest private collection of medieval prayer books outside of the United Kingdom. So I did what I had to do," I murmured.

"What do you mean, you did what you had to do? Your task was to verify the book's authenticity—which you did with remarkable ease, I might add—and then send the photographic proof on to Rosewood's lawyers. Nothing more."

"Retrieval has always been part of my arsenal, if I feel that it's the only viable option. Nobody ever questioned my judgment before I retired." I knew her words were not meant to sting, but they sure did, as badly as a handful of nettles.

My job at the Rosewood Agency could best be described as surveillance and reconnaissance. Under normal circumstances, getting the object back was someone else's problem and usually involved a team of lawyers. Yet, if I felt that the object in question might disappear or be destroyed before

Rosewood's legal team could act, then I was authorized to remove it from the premises. At least, my senior status had come with this perk before I retired three years ago. So what had changed?

"This is all my fault," the Baroness murmured. "I hadn't expected to you take it, merely photograph it. Otherwise, I would have caught you up sooner. But we were rushed to get here, and we had so much to catch up on. It never occurred to me...never mind. In light of recent developments, it might be better that the book was taken from you." She readjusted her tiara as she spoke, a telltale sign that she was not telling me everything she knew.

"What are you talking about, Sophie?"

My partner must have known that I was serious because I used her given name—something I rarely did. She shook her head and blinked three times, as if she was erasing our conversation from her memory.

"Never mind, we don't have time to go into all of it now, but suffice to say that there have been a few incidents since you retired." The words passed over her lips like a badly prepared meal. "Let's talk about it later. Right now, we have a more pressing concern—who killed Harold and stole his books?"

"I don't really care who did him in. To me, the more important question is: where are the illuminated manuscripts? There is only one door leading in or out of the library, and the only way off this floor is via the staircase, which is in clear view of the party. They are fragile, jewel-encrusted books—you just don't sling them under your arm and lug them about, at least not if you want them to retain their value."

"Are you certain the manuscripts aren't buried under the first editions?"

"How could they be? They were still in those display cases when the bookshelf fell on me. Which means whoever did this removed them after they'd pushed it over."

A sudden realization stopped my train of thought, causing me to chew on my lower lip. "He or she was taking a huge risk. The bookcase crashing to the floor must have made quite a bit of noise."

The Baroness shook her head. "I didn't hear a thing. The music was so loud, a truck could have driven through the hallway, and I wouldn't have heard it. And that curator would not stop babbling about his museum's own

COLLECTING CAN BE MURDER

meager collection of prayer books, so I was looking for any excuse to get out of there."

"If you didn't hear it fall over, why did you come to our aid?"

"You two were gone so long, Tammy began asking everyone where you'd gone. When I told her, she stormed off to find you. It was her scream that drew us to you."

"Interesting." I thought back on the display cases lining the walls of the library, partially hidden by the standing bookcases filling the room. How could our thief have gotten those fragile old books out of that room without anyone noticing? Moments later, a possibility entered my mind.

"Maybe the thief didn't need to move them far."

When the Baroness's eyebrows shot up, I added, "I have an idea of where they might be. Come on, I'll show you."

We exited the living room and entered the hallway. The space was shaped like a half moon, leaving an opening in the center of the home. A wide, spiral staircase made of dark-brown metal connected the floors, leading guests down to the entrance hall, or up to the bedrooms on the second and third floor.

"This staircase is only accessible from here, so anyone using it would be in plain view of the guests in the living room." I then nodded towards the neighboring dining room and attached kitchen. "As well as anyone walking along the hallway towards the dining room or kitchen. Wouldn't you agree?"

The Baroness examined the layout before responding, "Yes, I concur."

I glanced at the pastoral-themed tapestries dressing the curved concrete walls as we walked towards the library. The sweet scent of flowering hyacinths drew my eye to a gorgeous bouquet of fresh wildflowers in a crystal vase, resting on one of the most intricately decorated nineteenth-century French Boulle cabinets I'd ever seen. The inlaid bouquets of fantasy flowers and dancing figures gracing its surface pushed its value up past ten grand, I figured. In any case, it was certainly worth enough that someone should have placed a doily under that vase.

When we reached the library door, now closed, I whispered my theory to my partner as I jiggled the door handle as discreetly as I could. "I think the missing illuminated manuscripts are still in there. Our thief could have taken them out of the display cases and hidden them somewhere else in this room, possibly among the other books. It would have only taken a few minutes to move them, and then they could have returned to the party and no one would have been the wiser. They must be planning on removing the books from the house, once the storm passes."

I cupped my hand and looked into the darkened room through the glass-paned doors, hoping to see a telltale glint of silver or gold, but to no avail.

"If that's the case, then whoever did this is either family or works here," the Baroness stated.

"Why do you say that?"

"The door is locked, and only family members have a key, I believe. The thief would need to have easy access to the library, otherwise they would not be able to get the books out of the house without having to break in. Not everyone is as adept as you at picking locks."

I gently nudged her shoulder with mine. "You make a good point, partner."

My mind flew over the guest list. Most were wealthy art collectors, like the Baroness, who were here to see the illuminated manuscripts Harold was about to auction off. It wasn't simply kindness or a need to show off that made him extend this invitation to a select few. By inviting these art lovers over to his house for this exclusive party, he was hoping everyone present would be so enamored by the books that they would bid against each other and drive the prices up. It was a smart tactic, and one often used by those with a network of wealthy collector friends. Yet none of the guests would have easy access to Harold's library after the party was over—unless they were also good friends with our recently departed host.

From the conversations I had already overheard this evening, there were a few attendees who seemed to be closer to Harold than the rest. Billy Sanders had already declared himself to be an old friend of our host. Then there was Raven, Harold's moody daughter. She would certainly be able to gain access to the library after the party was over. Yet the other guests were still a mystery to me. During the party, Harold had hopped from group to group, as if he was afraid of leaving anyone out, but I didn't recall him talking longer to one person than another.

Before the Baroness and I could bat around ideas as to who took the books, our hostess clapped her hands together so loudly that it echoed through the hallway. As much as I admired the architecture, the extensive use of concrete and an open floor plan turned the entire house into an echo chamber.

When we shuffled back to the living room to see what was going on, Tammy was standing in front of the rest of the guests, seated before her.

"The police have been informed of Harold's death. The storm has felled a lot of trees between here and the station, so they are not able to respond right away. They did ask that we all remain inside tonight because it's not safe to travel."

One of the guests, a middle-aged man with his hair slicked back close to his skull, slammed his fist onto a side table.

"This is ridiculous! The police cannot require us to stay here. I am leaving." The man's thick French accent made his frustration sound adorable.

"No, you are not, Jack, so sit down and hush up." Tammy glared at him. "It's not safe to drive anywhere tonight."

"My home is only a three-hour drive from here," the Frenchman insisted. "I am an adult—if I wish to brave the weather, that's my choice."

"No, I'm afraid it's not that simple. The police made quite clear that no one was to leave, or I would be held responsible. They don't have enough manpower to deal with any more casualties tonight, and I don't want another death on my hands. One is enough. We have no choice but to stay inside until the storm passes."

She gazed around wearily. "There is plenty of room for everyone. That's one advantage of living in a such a large home—there's always room for guests, though it's going to cost a fortune to heat this place tonight. I can't wait to move away from this horrible house."

More murmurs of irritation and claims that they had to be somewhere else tonight were met with a shushing hand.

"I didn't make the rules, the police did, but I am going to enforce them." Tammy's snappy tone silenced the guests.

"My Harold is dead, and it may not have been an accident. Anyone

14

attempting to leave will be considered a suspect in my husband's murder. Thank you all for your attention. My housekeeping staff will show you to your rooms when you are ready."

A housekeeper who had been busy clearing dirty glasses from the living room, a plump woman who looked to be in her fifties, stepped forward. Tears splashed onto her cheeks and uniform. "Are you saying someone intentionally killed Harold?"

When Tammy nodded, the woman dropped the tray of empty glasses onto a table and sprinted off, wailing as she went.

The Baroness leaned in towards me. "Either that's a dedicated employee, or she and Harold were having an affair."

I studied our hostess while she watched her employee run off, her mind presumably running through the same possibility. Instead of stalking off after her, Tammy caught my eye and waved me over.

"What exactly were you doing with my husband in his library? You two snuck off so suddenly, I didn't have a chance to ask."

I threw my hands up to ward off her insinuation. "Nothing untoward, I assure you. As you know, I was interviewing him for *Hidden Treasures* magazine, and he graciously allowed me to photograph a few pages of his illuminated manuscripts for the article."

I spoke the truth, at least about staying virtuous. In my fifteen years on the job, I had never done anything I wouldn't tell my mother about. And *Hidden Treasures* was real, though my articles were always ghostwritten by a professional journalist. The magazine's healthy number of subscribers helped legitimize my cover.

"In point of fact, I did not know," Tammy growled. "None of this sounds like my Harold. If he was going to be interviewed, he would have told me."

I nodded, signaling that I understood her concern. "It all happened rather suddenly. I reached out to Harold when Lady Sophie informed me that we were going to be attending this private viewing, but he didn't seem interested in being interviewed. At least, not at first. But two days ago, he changed his mind and agreed to speak to me during the party."

"But you are here as the guest of the Baroness, not as a journalist," Tammy said accusingly, like she'd just trapped me in a lie.

"In fact, I am here in Europe to document Lady Sophie's buying spree for my magazine. My editor wants me to write a monthly column highlighting one of her recent purchases. But when I heard about Harold's illuminated manuscripts, I couldn't resist reaching out. His is exactly the kind of collection that the readers of *Hidden Treasures* are interested in."

My being the Baroness's "plus one" was our modus operandi. Her social network was so extensive—and she was so charming in her hoity-toity way—that she was an often-invited guest to parties so exclusive, only the most renowned socialites would know they were taking place.

Tammy's smirk dimmed slightly, as if she'd been one-upped. "Do you know why Harold changed his mind about the interview?"

"Not exactly. I only know that he was far more receptive to the idea after I explained how the extra publicity would help increase the collection's overall value, as well as ensure that everyone knew who held the largest collection of medieval prayer books outside of the United Kingdom. I can show you my notes and photographs if you don't believe me."

I stuck my hand into my Hermès Birkin bag, but didn't feel my notebook's stiff cover. But then again the purse was large and bulky. My possessions tended to disappear once inside. It was quite unbecoming for a proper lady to carry around something so big, but thankfully excusable for a fake journalist. I turned the gigantic bag over, confident that the chloroform spray was safely tucked into a zippered pocket hidden in the seam. Only after I dumped the contents—two pieces of chewing gum, a tieback for my long brown hair, a tube of maroon lipstick, a hairbrush full of strands, and a couple of pens—onto the marble top of a Louis XV marquetry commode worth about fifty thousand dollars was it clear to all present that neither were in there.

"Where are they?" I thought back to when I used my notebook and camera last, snapping my fingers as I realized when and where.

"They must still be in the library. I definitely had them with me when the bookcase fell over. Would you mind if I go look for them?"

Tammy's face drained of color. "Must you? I would rather my Harold not be disturbed."

"I really need them back, and not only because of the interview with Harold. I've taken many notes and photos documenting the Baroness's recent purchases, as well. Lady Sophie has been on the road for three weeks now, and that's a lot of information to lose."

Before I started working for Rosewood, I abhorred lying. Now it was part of my job description. The truth was, the Baroness and I had flown to Paris last night so that we could attend this party, as well as several others whose hosts might have stolen works in their private collections. With a little luck, we would have wrapped up a half dozen or so cases by the time our whirlwind trip around Europe was over.

When Tammy glared at me instead of answering, I added, "I'm also certain my editor will want to run this story about Harold as soon as he hears what has happened. As I said before, the publicity generated by this article will help increase the collection's overall value substantially."

Money signs seemed to light up in Tammy's eyes. "All right, I'll let you into the library, but make it quick, and don't touch my husband."

I placed my hand over my heart. "I won't, I swear."

4

Disturbing the Dead

Unfortunately, I had to break my promise to Tammy almost as soon as I entered the space. Sticking out from under one of poor Harold's legs was my notebook, recognizable thanks to the decent rendition of Vincent van Gogh's *Sunflowers* printed on its cover. As carefully as I could, I yanked the book loose. Despite his suffocating death, Harold still wore a tranquil expression.

How did my notebook get under his body? I wondered as I stood in the same spot I had been when the bookshelf fell over. My mind cast back to the moments before the incident. I had set my notebook and camera down so I could wrap up the Avron Book of Hours before putting it in my purse. Yet, the bookcase fell over before I could complete my task.

But where had I set them down exactly? I rubbed at the diminishing bump on my forehead, hoping it would somehow help sharpen my memory of the evening's events. My actions only left me with a dull ache to show for it.

I looked to where the two tufted green chairs and mahogany table had stood. The chair Harold had been sitting in, as well as the gorgeous table, had been crushed under the weight of the bookcase, still lying horizontal across the space.

What a waste of great furniture, I thought, as I took in the mess of splintered wood and torn fabric. Now that more books had been removed, I could see that Harold's body seemed to have been pushed to the right by the force of the toppling bookcase, for his corpse was half-strewn over the remains of the table.

That would explain why he landed on top of my notebook, I realized. Yet, there was no sign of my camera. Even though the bookshelf had been righted, there were still hundreds of first editions littering the scene. If my camera was under them, it was going to take a while to find it.

I turned my attention to the books scattered around the squished reading table, hoping my camera had landed close to the notebook. I grabbed a few hardbacks, stacking them into a neat pile behind me. Most of the volumes were worth a few hundred dollars, or even thousands, though that was peanuts in comparison to what a single illuminated manuscript was worth. The medieval texts were far rarer and almost never came on the market. Those who collected them tended to hold onto them until their deaths, usually leaving a valuable collection of books for their heirs to fight over. Some were donated to public museums, but those kinds of gifts were few and far between.

As I dug through the layers, a glistening of metal caught my eye. It appeared to be under a pile of hardbacks on my left. Could it be one of the missing illuminated manuscripts?

My hands worked double-time as I quickly cleared the books. Yet it seemed that every time I removed one, it dislodged several others that tumbled off of the pile and took its place. After shifting seemingly hundreds of them, I could finally touch the floor, albeit briefly. That's when my fingers wrapped around a tiny object with a sharp point. I held it to the light, admiring the precision with which the gold cufflink had been crafted. It was a spike made of gold, topped with an actual-sized dice. Each dot was an indent that appeared to be filled with a diamond flake.

I bit on my lip to stop myself from whistling. Whoever dropped this would definitely miss it. Roger was wearing gold cufflinks when he arrived, but I hadn't been close enough to see the design. If this was his, it could have flown off when he helped to lift the bookcase off of his father's body. The piece of jewelry was small enough that it could have fallen through the cracks between the books and landed on the floor.

However, I couldn't help but frown as I took in the location I'd found it in. If it had popped off of Roger's sleeve, it must have traveled an unusual path to reach its destination, I realized. Roger and the others had tried lifting the bookcase from the opposite side.

Yet its final destination was quite close to the display cases. But try as I might, I could not recall Roger standing anywhere close to the glass cases lining the back wall. His only concern was getting the shelving unit off of his father.

I pocketed the cufflink, wondering whether it was a clue or a red herring. Either way, it gave me an excuse to have a heart-to-heart with Roger.

I glanced at my watch, grimacing when I realized that I'd already been inside the library for thirty minutes and had yet to clear a square foot of fallen books. At this rate, I would be here all night, and I doubted Tammy would afford me that luxury.

So I decided to use my remaining time to inspect the display cases lining the back wall for clues, instead. Miraculously, they were completely unscathed. After a cursory examination, it was obvious that the five illuminated manuscripts were gone, but there was little else that the glass-enclosed spaces could tell me. I wasn't a field agent or cop, meaning I didn't have a fingerprint kit or lab at my disposal. My only resources were more virtual in nature.

The only thing that stood out was that there were books missing from each case. If the thief had wanted to take all twenty, it would have been smarter to clear out one case before moving on to the next. So why did they target those five?

Was this a robbery for hire—meaning a thief was recruited to steal a specific list of objects from Harold's home? That could be the situation here, I realized, though crimes like that were quite rare, and definitely didn't happen as often in real life as the movies liked to make out.

Perhaps there was another connection linking the five books. I would have to try to find out which volumes were missing, other than the Avron Book of Hours. The thought of my target's sudden disappearance made me growl. Out of the thousands of books in Harold's collection, the thief had to take that one.

I'd maneuvered my way to one of the freestanding bookshelves and was scanning the titles, hoping the missing prayer books had been shoved in amongst the rest, when the sharp crack of heels on the tile floor alerted me to Tammy's arrival.

I stepped away from the bookshelf, just as she strode inside. Her sour expression made her displeasure clear.

"Why are you still in here? Did you find your notebook and camera or not?"

"I did find my notebook, but my camera must be buried under the other books. I could stack them up for you, if you don't mind me being here a little longer…" My voice trailed off, knowing she wouldn't agree.

"You are not to touch anything else in this room. I want to know what you and Harold were talking about. Give that notebook to me." Tammy held out her hand.

A real journalist would never bow to such pressure, but my degree in journalism was as fake as the Baroness's pearl necklace. I handed over the notebook without question. Luckily, I had already filled the first few pages with notes about the other, fictitious, private viewings the Baroness had supposedly attended before we arrived at Villa Saint Marie earlier this evening.

The last few pages were filled with notes from my conversations with Harold, both those that had already taken place via email, and our brief conversation earlier in the evening.

After an excruciatingly long ten minutes, Tammy finally made eye contact. "I see no mention of why Harold withdrew the books from the auction. Did he tell you why?"

"No, I'm afraid not. I did ask him, but he danced around the question." I wasn't lying to her. Why Harold had chosen to withdraw the prayer books from the auction mere hours before this private viewing began was beyond me, because he had been tight-lipped as to the reasons why during our brief interview. Now, his lips were sealed—permanently.

"However, he did say it had something to do with the announcement he was going to make, after our interview. Do you know what he was planning on saying?"

"No, I do not." She locked eyes with me again, almost as if she were trying to stare into my soul. Whether her intense expression was meant to scare me or not, I could not say. Either way, after I finally blinked and conceded to her staring contest, she slammed the notebook shut and handed it back to me.

"If we find your camera, I will have one of my staff get in touch with you." Her tone made her words sound like a dismissal. If the roads had been clear outside, I'm certain she would have had her butler gather up my things and show me to the door.

She turned on her heel to leave, when my words made her stop in her tracks.

I pointed to the display cases. "I don't mean to be a bother, but it seems strange to me that the thief left so many of the illuminated manuscripts behind. It's almost like they had a shopping list of books to steal, before they entered. Harold said he kept the library door locked and only family has a key." I kept my expression neutral and my tone as casual as possible, letting my presumption hang in the air.

Tammy's eyes narrowed. "Neither my children or I did this, if that's what you are implying. And we weren't the only ones with access to them. Earlier this afternoon, before you and Lady Sophie arrived, Harold sat in the library so guests could view them at their leisure."

She waved her arms around the space. "As you can see, the books are not hidden away. Harold may not have sought the media's attention, but he did not make a secret of what he possessed. In fact, I would say he was quite boastful to his friends and acquaintances about his collection's contents. That's why he invited so many former business associates to the viewing, so he could show them off."

She stalked closer, getting into my personal space, her temper flaring up as quickly as an angry viper and with the same intensity. "You also knew about his collection, and you'd never met him. For all I know, you planned this interview so you could steal his books."

I pointed to the enormous bump on my forehead. "I was hurt, too."

Tammy leaned in close and hissed, "But you weren't killed, were you? How do I know this isn't some sort of setup?"

"Why would I set your husband up?" I put on my best "whatcha talking about" expression, choosing to go on the defensive, as well. She need not know how close she was to the truth.

"I don't know, but I don't want you in here." Tammy pointed to the door. "Get out."

5

Back in the Saddle

As soon as Tammy released me, I located my partner, sipping a merlot in the living room, and whisked her over to a dark corner so we could talk privately. Since Harold's death had been announced, the atmosphere had grown grim and most of the guests stood clustered together with those they knew, eyeing the rest suspiciously.

The Baroness shook her head to and fro as she checked that no one was listening in, her perfectly bobbed silver-blonde hair swishing across her neck with each turn. "Did you find the book?"

"No, but I didn't get the chance to thoroughly search the space before Tammy came in. I'll have to find a way to get back in there later, though it will take a few hours to really tear the room apart. He must have thousands of books stored in the floor-to-ceiling shelves. The five missing prayer books could be anywhere in there."

My partner leaned back on one heel, tapping her chin thoughtfully. "Are you certain they are still in the library? Could the thief have moved them to another location?"

It was a logical question, yet it burned my britches that we had to consider it. I hated admitting defeat or that I was in the wrong, but the Baroness had taken a gamble by asking me back. "I don't know. They could have. I do know that this is not how this weekend was supposed to go. All I want to do is find that blasted book and get out of here."

Had I been out of the game too long? Before quitting, I had been one of Rosewood's best recovery specialists. I had taken a sudden and early retirement three years ago, after my husband had been murdered while attempting to recover antiques from a high-ranking member of the Italian Mafia. Or at least, my employer and I assumed that was what had happened. My husband's body had never been found, meaning I had to bury a box of rocks, instead.

Had my lack of recent experience colored my judgment, or even impaired it in some way? Had I overreacted tonight by drugging Harold and by taking the manuscript, and had my actions somehow set off this chain of events that led to his demise?

When I looked at my partner, self-doubt flooded my soul. "Am I losing my touch, Baroness? Whoever pushed over the bookcase snuck up on Harold and me."

I hung my head, hoping she couldn't see my reddening cheeks. "It's been so long since I've been out in the field, maybe I've gotten rusty. You may have made a mistake by asking me to be your partner on this assignment."

"Nonsense!" the Baroness protested. "You were the first person I thought of after my original partner backed out at the last minute."

The fact that her original partner's father had been diagnosed with terminal cancer and wanted to see his daughter once more before he passed seemed to have slipped the Baroness's mind. As much as I liked her, empathy was not one of her strong points.

Still, the Baroness had always been one of my favorite partners, so when she called and hesitantly asked me to help her out with this mission to locate several stolen objects during a whirlwind tour of Europe, I couldn't say no. Luckily, I had kept fit by teaching women's self-defense classes at the YMCA, and seeing as we never carried weapons, I didn't have much more training to catch up on. Not having children or a husband to tie me down meant I could leave at a moment's notice.

But who was I kidding? Her timing could not have been better. After three years of mourning my husband, it was time to get back in the game. I was fifty-two years old, not eighty-two, and early retirement did not suit me. I wasn't quite ready to fill my days with knitting, bingo, and water aerobics.

"From what our boss tells me, you didn't have much choice. You needed a quick fill-in and no other agents were available."

"That may be true, but I am still glad that you were able and willing to step out of retirement to join me on this tour. You know how much it means to me, being able to help others find their lost heirlooms. But I had expected you to be more keen to solve the mystery. Have you lost your appetite for it?"

Solving mysteries was part of my job, but usually those involved missing objects—not murders. My employer, a little-known company called the Rosewood Agency, specialized in the kinds of art loss cases that no other organization was willing or able to solve. Most of those who approached us for help were the directors of museums and galleries located around the world, hoping we could locate the pieces stolen from them.

The Rosewood Agency was the brainchild of Reginald Pinky Taylor Rosewood—or Reggie to his friends and employees. My boss was the hyper-intelligent founder of several successful technology-driven companies, with a private art collection to rival that of the Metropolitan Museum of Art. After several of his paintings were pilfered and the cops had no luck tracing the thieves or artwork down, my billionaire boss created his own network of professionals to investigate the crime. His top-notch team was composed of the best art recovery specialists and researchers money could buy—and in Reggie's case, that meant the absolute cream of the crop.

After they had successfully tracked down and recovered almost all of his stolen property, Reggie saw no point in disbanding his merry bunch of freelancers, so he began discreetly offering their services to other cultural organizations in need. Rosewood's databases were soon full of missing items, and the small team had to expand exponentially in order to keep up with all of the research and legwork needed to check the plethora of incoming leads.

I was part of the third round of hires, brought in to verify objects that had been traced to a certain owner or location. Because I spoke fluent Italian and Spanish, I was a good fit for the European team.

The vast majority of our leads came in through our ICT department. After the missing object was entered into the company's databases, the agency's computer nerds set up a spiderweb of internet alerts that pinged them whenever a reference to that object was discovered online. It was shocking how often a stolen work appeared in a gallery's website, an online auction catalog, or a seller's website such as eBay. Other leads came in as tips via a network of trusted contacts working at cultural institutions around the world.

In rare cases, we were able to find a lead to a missing work the week it was entered into our databases. However, it typically took months, or even years, for a missing object to surface again. Experience had taught me that the longer it took, the more likely the object had changed hands so often that it had been whitewashed of its dubious provenance. The current owner usually had no idea that their cherished painting, sculpture, or book was actually a stolen item.

As soon as an object did surface, the next step was to verify that it was indeed the same one that we sought. No matter how solid the lead, before we publicly humiliated a wealthy patron of the arts by accusing them of harboring something stolen, we had to be one hundred percent certain the person really did possess the object in question, as well as learn more about how they acquired it. Computers couldn't verify a find based on a keyword or photograph, nor could they tell if the person knew they were buying a stolen object, or thought it was clean. That took a personal touch—and usually a woman's.

That's where Rosewood's art sleuths, such as myself, came into play. At least, that's what I call myself. Technically I'm not a detective or private investigator, simply because I don't have my license. My actual job title—fine arts and antiques recovery specialist—is a mouthful and sounds boring at parties. Not that I go to many during which I can reveal my true identity. I usually only attend black-tie events as the Baroness's "plus-one."

Being an art sleuth on retainer was not a particularly well-paid job, when one considered the value of the works I was helping to recover, but did come with lots of cushy benefits that more than made up for the salary. I was particularly fond of traveling first class, and I know the Baroness loved the luxurious hotels they usually put us up in.

My art history background and martial arts expertise made me an ideal candidate for this position. Unfortunately, I didn't have the natural charisma, gigantic bank account, or extensive social network unique to old money that would have granted me casual access to the art lovers we suspected of owning stolen items. That's where the Baroness came in.

Lady Sophie Rutherford used her title and status as an obscenely rich art collector to get me into parties and homes that would normally never be open to someone like me. Among her wealthy friends, the Baroness was known for her catty conversation, well-informed gossip, and exquisite taste in art, which was why they welcomed her.

Yet to most outsiders, she came across as a snobbish witch who lived far above most people's means and treated those beneath her as rubbish on her heel. Her penchant for wearing ball gowns and a diamond-studded tiara didn't help her blend in with the common folk.

Our paths crossed a few years ago when I was asked to accompany the Baroness on her first mission. After the Rosewood Agency helped her recover a portrait of her then-recently deceased husband that had been stolen from their mansion, she had approached our boss and asked whether she could be of assistance. That first assignment was a test to see whether she could be useful to the agency.

My habit of calling her "Baroness" instead of "Lady Sophie" was a remnant from that first job—the recovery of an antique necklace that quickly spun out of control. Her hoity-toity manners grated on my nerves so badly, I had used her title improperly to irritate her back. After we managed to recover the jewelry by cooperating, our mutual respect grew and the next time I was assigned to work with her, I didn't grumble or file a complaint. But the name stuck, and instead of being an insult, she now regarded "Baroness" as my nickname for her.

I will admit, during those first few assignments, I was not entirely certain that we were a good match. I'm as clumsy as she is regal. Yet opposites seem to attract, or at least allow us to fill in each other's strengths and weaknesses. She's sharper and wittier than anyone gives her credit for, and I can imagine she enjoys helping solve any mysteries that cross our path, as a mental exercise. Not that she has ever said as much. Most of our conversations revolved around the current assignment, and not much else. I wouldn't call us friends, but I did come to enjoy her company during our missions.

Once she got me close to our target, it was my job to handle the rest, in a way that ensured her name and status remained unscathed. Armed with only my wits, chloroform spray, and a black belt in karate, I was tasked with verifying that the object in question was indeed the one we sought, as well as documenting its current state and location—preferably with photographic evidence.

Before my retirement, I had specialized in verifying the more urgent cases—paintings and sculptures that, for one reason or another, Rosewood's researchers suspected were probably going to disappear quite soon.

Which is why the Baroness thought to call me when she needed a last-minute fill-in. The Avron prayer book had been taken from a museum in Ohio ten years ago and vanished into thin air, which made its move from a low priority to one of the highest urgency, within minutes of the new tip coming in to the Rosewood Agency, rather unique.

Our tipster was a wealthy socialite who had hosted several parties I'd attended over the years as the Baroness's guest, which made her a credible informant. She also collected rare literature, which was why she'd attended a sale of several book collections at an obscure auction house in Switzerland a month ago. During it, she thought she recognized the Avron prayer book as being one that Rosewood was searching for.

Unfortunately, the book had already been shipped to the buyer by the time my employer's lawyers were able to contact the auction house. After a few conversations with our legal team, its director finally allowed us to see the paperwork the seller had brought in, which proved the medieval prayer book had been in his family for generations. It was fake, of course, as was the name and contact information of the supposed grandson who had claimed to have inherited the illuminated manuscript.

After that, the director had willingly shared with Rosewood's lawyers the name and address of the buyer—Harold Moreau of Villa Saint Marie, just outside of Tréflaouénan, France. The auction house director's only request was that we not tell Harold how we had learned that he had recently purchased the book.

Considering the auction house employees didn't know that the manuscript was stolen because they had failed to perform due diligence before selling it, I doubted Harold knew about the book's nefarious history, either. Yet, it was my job to find out for certain.

Once we knew who to target, several of the well-connected art lovers working for the Rosewood Agency set about figuring out a way to get close to the buyer. Luckily for us, Harold had already announced a private viewing of his illuminated manuscripts collection, part of which he was planning on auctioning off through a Parisian auction house. Though the guest list was quite exclusive, it didn't take more than a single, well-placed phone call for the Baroness to be invited to attend.

Harold's book of hours was our first stop, and I wanted to do everything possible to make certain this mission was a success. I needed that boost of self-confidence to keep going. Perhaps more importantly, I needed to know that I could do my job without having to look over my shoulder the entire time, in fear of my life. No one had known that the man who murdered my husband was really a high-ranking Mafia figure. According to our intel, he was just one of the many rich Italian collectors Rosewood suspected of harboring stolen objects. Otherwise Carlos never would have tried to get a closer look at the antiques the man had in his possession. But that stroke of bad luck had gotten my husband killed, and I didn't want to constantly worry the same thing would happen to me.

"Earth to Carmen—can you hear me?" My partner's snobby voice cut through my thoughts.

"You asked if I have lost my appetite for solving mysteries. I certainly hope not because one just landed in our laps." My spine straightened as my resolve to find the book strengthened. "The prayer book must still be somewhere in this house."

As if to remind me to get back to work, lightning lit up the sky, seconds before a tree limb crashed against the side of the villa. The ceiling lamps flickered, but held.

"It sounds like the police weren't lying about the storm. I guess that means we'll have plenty of time to search the house tonight. What do you say we get to it?"

6

Toasting or Roasting

We tiptoed downstairs only to find Tammy, Raven, Roger, and Billy the museum curator gathered in the library, toasting Harold. There may have been more guests inside, but those were the only people I could see reflected in the open door's glass panels.

The Baroness and I leaned over the railing curving around the half-moon hallway and watched the storm raging outside. My body was positioned so I could watch the reflections inside the library without staring at the highly polished doors. What we really needed was a drink to complete the setup, but I was afraid I would draw Tammy's attention to the hallway if I walked back to the party to get us refreshments. Luckily, their voices reverberated out into the hallway, making it easy to eavesdrop.

In the reflection, I could see Roger raising a glass. "To Harold, one of the world's most successful toy salesmen."

"That's a strange way to toast your dad," I whispered to the Baroness.

Tammy's reaction was too soft to hear, but Raven's laugh and Billy's indignant reaction were not.

"Hey, I thought we are here to toast Harold, not roast him," the curator said.

"I would say that Roger was spot on—Dad cared more about his stupid toys than us," Raven added, rage coloring her voice.

"I forgot, in your eyes Harold could do no wrong—right, Billy? Say, you never did tell me why you are here this weekend. I know your museum can't afford any of his prayer books." The accusatory tone of Tammy's taunting insult was not lost on me. But why would she be angry with the curator?

When Billy remained silent, she prodded further. "Why did Harold fly you over from Boston?"

"He, um, had a surprise for me, I'm not sure how much I should say..." Billy's voice trailed off before it rose again. "Have you found his will yet?"

"No, but then I haven't had a chance to look." Tammy's voice was full of suspicion. "But why would Harold's last wishes be any concern of yours? He wouldn't have left your museum anything."

"I wouldn't be so sure about that." Billy's tone had a self-assuredness I'd not yet heard from the mustached curator.

"What are you implying?" Tammy snarled.

I leaned forward instinctively, wishing I could be a fly on the wall inside of the library just to see their expressions, when the discreet patter of soft-soled shoes approaching fast made me whip around, instead.

Behind us stood Jeeves, the butler. "Can I show you to your rooms? Or is there anything else you require this evening?"

Despite his eyes being a bit red, his back remained straight and his facial expression passive. Seeing as how it was well past midnight and thus more night than evening, I could imagine the poor fellow just wanted to go to bed. He didn't seem interested in why we were standing outside of the library, only in fulfilling our wishes so he could clock out for the night.

Unfortunately, his questions caused Tammy to rush towards us, stopping in the library's threshold, panic in her voice. "Who's there?"

I strode forward, as if I was walking towards the library and hadn't been standing outside the door for the last few minutes, listening in.

Tammy's arms folded over her torso when she spotted me and the Baroness.

I peeked my head through the doorway and noted the guests present inside. "Tammy! I apologize for disturbing you. You'd asked everyone to stay out of the library, but we heard voices when we were going upstairs to bed, so we thought we would investigate. But it's your house and you are obviously busy, so we'll let you be."

"Alright. Goodnight." Her glare and posture made clear that she didn't believe a word I'd said. She kicked the door closed with her heel and returned to the library table, around which Harold's children and Billy were seated.

As we retreated, I bit my lip, wishing my employer-provided toolkit included a more extensive surveillance system. Unfortunately, my boss seemed to think that pesky privacy concerns and the risk of me getting caught violating them outweighed any possible benefits. Instead, I had to make do with a digital SLR camera—now missing and presumed broken—and my smartphone.

When we approached the living room, I noticed that the music was turned way down and the few voices we could hear were quite slurred. From the hallway, I spotted the three remaining guests all leaning against the makeshift bar with their eyes half-closed.

"I doubt they are going to tell us anything useful." Instead of entering, I continued on towards the staircase. "I guess we can try to get into the library later tonight."

The Baroness's hand flew to her mouth as she tried to hide her yawn. She then glanced at her watch, its tiny analog face worked into a jewel-encrusted bracelet. "It's already one in the morning and the party is over. If we go back to search the library later and someone catches us, it would look awfully suspicious. Perhaps early tomorrow morning would be better? Nobody is going anywhere tonight, thanks to the storm."

"I suppose you're right." I tried, yet failed, to keep the disappointment out of my voice. "I just hope we can figure out where the Avron book is before the police arrive. After they interview us, we will have no reason to be here."

My partner laid a hand on my arm. "Even if we don't retrieve it, you have already proven that Harold had the stolen prayer book in his possession. So in fact, we have successfully completed our first assignment, even if we don't know exactly where the book is presently at."

I bit my lip and turned away, hoping the Baroness couldn't see the frustration etched on my face. "You're right, but it would be wonderful to hand the book over to the US Embassy in Paris, instead of having to pass the case off to Rosewood's lawyers."

My partner tittered softly, the rubies in her earrings catching in the light. "My darling Carmen, dealing with the retrieval is the lawyers' job and why they are paid such hefty retainer fees. We get the parties and glamour, and they get to clean up the mess."

"Then that's it for tonight," I said with a sigh. As if trying to summon me upstairs, my head began to pound ever so slightly, reminding me that I had suffered a nasty blow and was still not one hundred percent healthy.

The Baroness began climbing the stairs. "We will both think more clearly after a good night's sleep. The subconscious is a mysterious thing. With a little luck, the killer's true identity will be revealed in our dreams."

7

A Shoulder To Cry On

My partner and I headed upstairs, our heels clicking on the metal treads of the winding staircase. Even without the head injury, I wouldn't have wanted to whip up or down these too fast for fear of getting dizzy.

As we passed the second-floor landing on our way up to the third floor, a heart-wrenching sob made me stop and listen. "What was that?"

The Baroness rolled her eyes. "None of our business, is what it is."

I smirked at my partner before tiptoeing into the hallway. As much as I liked her as a person, my partner was not a touchy-feely person and had trouble with open displays of emotions—two traits that ended up driving a wedge between us after my husband died. Perhaps her English father's "stiff upper lip" attitude towards life had rubbed off on her. Or maybe she just wasn't wired like that.

Whatever the reason, her inability to show compassion made her a no-show at my husband's funeral, precisely where I needed her shoulder to cry on. Our friends and family didn't know what kind of work Carlos and I did for the Rosewood Agency, which meant they couldn't know the real reason why I had no body to bury. As far as they were concerned, the ocean liner he had gone down on had sunk to such a low spot on the Atlantic seabed, it could not be recovered. I had needed someone by my side who knew what I was really going through, not that charade I had to play for the rest. But she had let me down.

That was three years ago. We hadn't spoken since, until she called a few days ago, asking whether I would be willing and able to fly to Paris and help her out with a job. Unfortunately, neither one of us had yet dared to broach the subject of Carlos's funeral, and I suspected that if I wanted to hash it out with her, I would have to be the one to begin the conversation. I just wasn't quite ready to open up that can of worms, not when I was trying to find my feet again.

Our boss had made clear that I was back on freelance-basis only, simply because he wasn't certain I was mentally fit enough to handle the work again. I needed the Baroness on my side, if I was going to worm my way back into the Rosewood Agency on a more consistent basis. At least, if I wanted to go back to sleuthing full time. How things went during this trip would help me decide what the future held.

As I made my way down the hall, a second heart-wrenching sob drew me closer to the source—the third door on my right. Before the Baroness could stop me, I knocked on it.

A shuffling noise on the other side told me that whoever it was had heard me. Yet it seemed like an eternity before a hesitant voice asked, "Who's there?"

"It's Carmen De Luca, the journalist who was interviewing Harold before he died. Are you alright? I thought I heard crying."

A few sniffles followed, before the door handle turned and the room's occupant peered out through a small crack. It was the housekeeper who had burst into tears upon hearing about Harold's death. She didn't appear to be faring much better now, based on how red and puffy her eyes were. With her hair hanging loose around her shoulders, instead of tied up tight in her constrictive bun, she looked even younger and more fragile.

"Hello, Carmen. I'm Simone. That's kind of you to ask. Please, come inside." She stepped back and opened the door further.

"Maybe she was his mistress," the Baroness murmured as she passed by me to enter.

If so, Harold had a much broader taste in women than I would have suspected. Simone and Tammy couldn't have been more different. Simone hadn't worn makeup earlier, let alone now, whereas Tammy had enough products on that she could open her own beauty supply store. Simone's mousy brown hair looked to have been lopped off by a pair of kitchen scissors, instead of having been perfectly colored and coifed by a stylist. Her uniform was a bland black and white ensemble required by her employer, which was not tailored. So it was no surprise that it was a tight squeeze for such a short and plump woman. Yet her current selection—a floral-print muumuu with nothing on underneath—was also not a frock Tammy would be caught dead in.

Once the door shut again, Simone let the floodgates open, and soon she was dripping tears and snot onto her tiny bed's duvet. I grabbed a box of Kleenex and shoved it under her nose, hoping to catch the worst of it. The Baroness stood with her back stiff-straight against the door, as far away as she could get from Simone without leaving the room.

When I realized the housekeeper wasn't going to stop crying of her own volition, I inquired, "What's got you so upset?"

"Harold is dead!" she wailed as her body became racked with sobs once again.

"It is tough when someone you know dies." I patted her shoulder softly as we waited for an explanation. Behind Simone, an old photo album was open on the pillow. Based on the outfits and hairstyles, the tattered pages held her childhood memories.

When the housekeeper's tears showed no sign of abating, I knew the Baroness wouldn't stay much longer, so I decided on a more direct approach. "You seem awfully upset about Harold's death. Were you two having an affair?"

I didn't really care who was sleeping with whom, but I did want to get this situation resolved so the Baroness and I could get to bed. Tomorrow was going to be a busy day, and it was awfully late.

The middle-aged woman startled and stared at me, as if I had slapped her. At least she'd stopped crying. "Of course not! He was a good boss, that's all." She wiped off her tears with a handful of tissues, and once her face and hands were mostly dry, she twisted around and grabbed the photo album.

"It's the first anniversary of my mother's death." Simone stroked the photos lovingly as she spoke. "And Harold dying on the same day is bringing back all sort of nasty memories. I really miss her."

"What happened to her?" My voice was a whisper. Simone had unwittingly found the crack in my armor—my mother.

"She died of cancer. We didn't have enough money for treatment so it ate away at her until there was nothing left. At least Harold died fast and didn't have to suffer like Maman did. And here he had all this money. If I had only known…" A dark cloud passed over her face as her words hung in the air.

I gulped back a tear; Simone's words brought back so many horrible memories of my mother's last days. I knew too well the pain of watching a parent slowly slip away before your eyes. It wasn't cancer that took her life, but a drunk driver who left her body shattered and her brain irreversibly injured. That she slipped into a coma and never regained consciousness was my only consolation.

"What about your father? Is he still in the picture?"

Simone's eyes squeezed close as she shook her head. "He never was. Maman was everything to me—my parents, provider, and advisor."

Her words were like a punch in the gut; our conversation was starting to feel like therapy. I made a point of examining the photos until I got my emotions back under control. Seeing that tattered old album, with its little hooks holding those squares of faded memories, brought back all sorts of recollections of my own family, most of whom I only knew through old photographs.

"That's really rough," I finally managed to say. I wasn't just being polite—I knew firsthand how tough it was to never know a parent, to have that gaping hole in your family history that no one could fill. Thanks to years of therapy, I finally learned that losing a parent so early shapes your soul, no matter whether you are aware of it.

My dad had died before I was born and thanks to an unresolved feud between his family and Mom's, my mother put a whole lot of distance between me and them. Not that I'm looking for pity; Mom's side of the family more than made up for it. I never wanted for love, attention, or toys.

My grandma even moved in to help raise me when I hit puberty and blamed Mom for everything. Thank goodness that glorious old girl is still alive and kicking.

Simone toyed with the hem of her muumuu. "She never admitted it, but it broke her heart that he left her. She never did date another man because she'd always said he was the love of her life, but the feeling was not reciprocated. That's why she finally took me to Paris, so her mother could help raise me."

"Wow, if you were raised in Paris, how the heck did you find out about this place? I can't believe it was the only villa in France hiring housekeepers."

Simone chuckled, hiding her lopsided grin with the back of her hand. "It is indeed in the middle of nowhere, as you Americans say. Maman worked as housekeeper here for one summer. That's how I knew about it. Her descriptions made it sound like such a magical place, full of love and laughter. I've been curious about it ever since, which is why I responded to their advertisement for a housekeeper. But whatever Maman saw in it is no longer here."

I glanced at the pictures while she dried the latest round of tears. Though the decades-old photos had bleached out and were a little blurry, one of the women stood out as a strong candidate for Simone's mother. I pointed to a faded image, the name "Cherie" scrawled underneath in loopy letters.

"Is that your mother? You two could have been twins."

"So many people say that! That's her. My middle name is Cherie, so I feel as if I carry her with me wherever I go." Simone smiled slightly before sharing another story about her beloved mother. I gazed over the photos of them in Parisian parks and in front of the Louvre pre-pyramid, while I listened attentively. Her memories reminded me of mine, and we continued to swap stories of our childhoods until the Baroness's yawns became constant.

As we said our goodnights, I couldn't help but hug Simone. Our common bond made me want to protect her, as much as comfort her. It had been a long time since I'd met someone with whom I felt an instant kinship. My best friend, Rhonda, was really the only other one. And Simone's more difficult upbringing reminded me of how things could have gone, if my mother's large family hadn't been glad to help raise me.

After we climbed the last flight of stairs and were back inside of our room, I turned to the Baroness. "I'm going to set my alarm for six a.m. so I can get down to the library before everyone else wakes up."

"That sounds like a splendid plan."

"Do you want to join me or sleep in?" I asked, already knowing the answer.

The Baroness gave me one of her over-the-nose looks as she replied, "Join you, of course. One can only take so many society parties before they begin to tire. That's why I sign up for these assignments, to get my adrenaline fix for the year."

8

Hello, Billy!

As large as Harold's house was, there were more than a dozen guests sleeping over, so the Baroness and I were sharing a room. Luckily, the space was as large as my entire apartment, and the two king-sized beds were separated by a screen divider made of painted silk so long that it practically split the room in two. I took in the chipped wooden frame, figuring the wear and tear would bring the price down to the low thousands. Still, this was one of a dozen guest rooms. The attention to detail she'd given it illustrated that Tammy had spared no expense when decorating this massive house.

When the Baroness retreated to the bathroom, I stretched out on my bed, certain I wouldn't be able to sleep. I was too wired after my conversation with Simone and my mind too full of memories that I didn't want to recall at the moment.

Besides, I wanted to take a steaming hot bath, and I knew my partner was going to be awhile. It took a lot of cleaners and moisturizing products to maintain her pristine appearance. I had time to kill.

So instead of getting lost in childhood what-ifs, I grabbed my laptop to see what else I could find out about our fellow guests. I had already looked up Harold and his wife before flying over, as well as a few of the other invited collectors he had name-dropped during our email exchanges. Despite my attempts to wheedle it out of him, Harold was reluctant to share the entire guest list with me. My posing as a journalist may have had something to do with it.

The Baroness knew several of the guests superficially from parties and charity events, but she wasn't privy to their darkest secrets, which could be a reason to murder our host. It was up to me and my company-assigned ICT specialist to find out what they didn't want everyone to know.

As a senior agent, I had a direct line to the most talented nerd of the bunch—Myrtle Rosewood, a seventy-something computer whiz who could hack the virtual pants off of a teenager any day. Yet, as talented as she was at infiltrating governmental agencies and general espionage, it was not a pleasure to work with her. She had the mouth of a sailor and the manners of a raging bull. Worst of all, she loved to condescend to me as if I was a junior agent new to the field, even after fifteen years of working together. Yet there was no point in complaining; her job was secure for life simply because she was mother to my boss, Reggie Rosewood.

When I was out on this assignment, Myrtle was my only backup, save for the Baroness. Yet it was my job to ensure that my lady friend's dainty hands remained clean of anything that could be deemed illegal. A Baroness with a criminal record was of no use to the agency.

Before I sicced Myrtle on them, though, I wanted to get to know our guests better. The presence of Harold's son and daughter was a surprise, simply because I hadn't expected our host to invite family to a business party. For that reason, I started with them.

I soon learned that Roger was a professional gambler living in Las Vegas. From the many articles I could find about the thirty-one-year-old's rapid rise to the top of the circuit, it seemed he had had a promising start, after having won several important tournaments and big cash prizes. However, his luck took a turn for the worse about a year ago, and there were rumors of drug abuse and looming bankruptcy. After he returned to the circuit two months ago, presumably now clean and definitely flush with cash, his comeback had not been spectacular, but rather bumpy at best.

I made a note to have Myrtle dig deeper into his past. If there was anything naughty to find out about Roger, my company-assigned computer nerd would discover it; of that I was certain.

Next, I took a look at Raven. Harold's daughter from his previous marriage was fifteen years older than her half brother. She had founded a promising startup that did something with wind energy and solar panels that I didn't quite understand—technology was never my strong suit—but it looked like one of those new green-energy companies that were in fashion these days. Splashed across her website was a news release announcing a major expansion and teasers hinting that Raven was about to take her company public.

Before I could email Myrtle to ask her to look into the siblings' backgrounds, a noise in the hallway made me cock my head to better listen. Was someone singing "Hello, Dolly"? I sprung off the bed and lay my ear on the wooden door. It sounded like Billy the curator was singing the showtune in an off-key voice as he stumbled up the metal staircase. An odd choice at two in the morning, in a hallway full of sleeping guests.

Apparently I wasn't the only one whose rest he had disturbed, for when I opened the door a crack to see if he was alright, I noted several strips of light coming from other rooms up and down the hallway. Luckily for Billy, he wasn't alone.

"Nothing to see here folks," Roger said jovially. "Billy had a little too much to drink, that's all. I'll get him to bed, and everyone can get the rest they deserve. Sorry for disturbing your sleep."

He had his arm around Billy's waist and was half-dragging the portly man down the hallway to his room. Billy, in turn, was attempting to perform a high-kick as he belted out the chorus. Tammy scurried around her son and opened the bedroom door for them.

As soon as Roger carried the singing curator inside, Tammy glanced back into the hallway and shrugged before slamming the door shut.

"We've all been there," I mumbled as I returned to bed to complete my email to Myrtle.

As much as I hated having to fill her in on our progress so far, I was obliged to tell my company contact that I had verified the Avron book as being the stolen object Rosewood was searching for, moments before it vanished again. It was that last bit that stuck in my craw. It didn't help that my photographic evidence had been presumably destroyed at the same time. With a little luck, Rosewood's lawyers could still spring into action, but I had my doubts.

However, I did not mention that I had been in the process of pocketing the Avron book when the bookcase fell, figuring it wasn't important for her to know. Having the book taken from me in that way would make me look like an amateur, and I didn't want to give Myrtle more fuel to throw on the fire. She already treated me as a rookie, as it was.

I'd just hit send when the Baroness opened the bathroom door, a wave of steam announcing her return. She was swathed in a fluffy white bathrobe with a matching towel wrapped around her head like a turban.

"That bubble bath is sensational. I feel like a new woman." Lady Sophie sighed contently and sank down into one of the plush armchairs before wagging a French-manicured finger at me. "I knew you couldn't resist—you've been investigating our guests, haven't you?"

I laughed. "You got me there. I looked into Roger's and Raven's backgrounds, but have found nothing untoward. At least, not worth murdering for."

"What kind of people are they?"

I shared what little I'd found, and mentioned emailing Myrtle to see what she could dig up about both siblings. I knew I should have held my tongue when the Baroness's lips curled downwards.

"I would have preferred to have kept her out of this, for as long as possible."

Neither would tell me what exactly happened during my absence, but it was clear the two stubborn women wanted nothing to do with each other. Which was strange considering they had been the best of friends before I retired. All I knew for certain was that that their squabbling had gotten so out of hand, the owner of the Rosewood Agency had been forced to intervene.

Both women were given the choice to either quit or figure out a way to work together. From the few tidbits I could get out of the Baroness, Sophie blamed Myrtle for whatever had happened and was not pleased with Reggie's intervention or ultimatum. Considering Myrtle was his mother, I could imagine the Baroness found him to be unfairly partial to his family. Neither had given Reggie their notice, and both had been outdoing each other in sweetness ever since. I could tell all that fake civility was getting on the Baroness's nerves.

My partner ignored my mention of Myrtle, and instead we spent a few minutes considering Harold's kids as suspects in his murder. It didn't take us long. Despite his arrogant attitude and serial-killer charm, Roger had arrived after the body had been found, ruling him out as a potential murderer. And Raven didn't seem interested in anything except her business.

After assessing the situation and our possible options, we finally reached two conclusions: firstly, neither one of us really cared who bumped Harold off. And as nice as it would have been to have retrieved the Avron prayer book, thereby successfully completing our first assignment, continuing to search for it was not worth getting mixed up in a murder investigation for.

Unfortunately, the weather wasn't on our side. Until the roads and train tracks could be cleared of fallen trees, we were stuck here. Tammy's threat to treat anyone who left as a suspect only made me feel more trapped.

When the Baroness reached for her eye shade, I knew she was ready to hit the sack.

"Goodnight," I said before turning off the overhead light and walking to the bathroom.

"Sweet dreams," she replied as she pulled the shade over her eyes and snuggled into bed.

I washed off the thick slab of makeup I'd applied before the party, scrubbing until my ruddy skin was once again visible. There's something so suffocating about foundation; I tried to avoid wearing it at all costs. As inviting as the tub looked, I was too tired to wait until it filled, so I skipped a bath in favor of dental hygiene. A quick brush and floss of the teeth, and I was ready to join the Baroness in slumberland.

Before I could reach my bed, more creaks from the stairs and hallway drew me back to the door.

"They need peepholes," I muttered as I tightened the bathrobe, then pulled the door open a smidgen.

Roger had just passed by our room, a large silver platter in his hands. It was one of those old-fashioned ones with a domed cover to keep the food warm. He had missed dinner and was presumably suffering from jet lag, so he must have been really hungry, I reckoned.

He ignored me and the shaft of light my open door must have produced, instead continuing on to his room and softly closing the door behind him.

Bon appétit, I thought before locking our door and crawling into bed.

I lay down on the feather-filled mattress and cast my mind back to the party. Maybe there was a clue to solving this mess in my conversation with Harold, just before he died. It was too bad that I couldn't hypnotize myself. Right now, I was willing to try anything. I could really use this win to keep my motivation up. Yet, before I could recall anything useful, I slipped into sleep.

9

Dancing the Night Away

Thankfully my dreams did my bidding, and soon I was back at the party, reliving Harold's final moments...

"Thanks for the invitation. This is quite the party," I said to our host, Harold Moreau, after he offered me a glass of wine. I let my tongue roll over the vintage red, savoring the hints of cedar and cinnamon, before smiling demurely up at him.

"I'm glad you're enjoying yourself. It is a pleasure to finally meet Lady Sophie—and fortunate that you were already on your way to my humble chateau, precisely at the moment that I decided to seek publicity for my collection."

Luck had nothing to do with it, I thought as I took another drink of my wine, this one a bit larger. Light jazz music, the kind I despised, played in the background, partially masking the sound of rain pounding against Harold's home on the Breton coast. We had feasted on a typically French meal—escargot and fresh greens, followed by a succulent lamb roast—but the protein-based meal hadn't quite settled in my stomach, I realized, as I held up a hand to hide a soft burp from the rest.

We were all gathered together in the living room, nursing our cocktails while waiting for our host to grant each of us a private viewing of his prized collection of medieval prayer books, also known as illuminated manuscripts.

The books were our reason for being here.

I studied the others over the rim of my wine glass. A dozen or so conservatively dressed middle-agers mingled, chatting softly and laughing at each other's catty remarks. But from their stiff body postures and stilted conversations, it was obvious that few knew each other well. My guess was the majority of invitees were business relations of Harold's, not actual friends who would have seen each other on a regular basis. Based on their accents, most were from the States, as well.

This select group was the kind one would expect to bid on rare manuscripts worth up to a million dollars apiece. Based on the flashes of diamond-studded jewelry, meters of silk and satin, gallons of expensive perfume, and abundance of meticulously tailored suits, I estimated that most of the guests were also worth at least a million apiece. They were the culture lovers among the jet set—an eclectic mix of nouveau riche and old money who tended to pop up whenever there was an interesting private viewing or auction going on.

This was definitely not my kind of get-together, but then again, I was here to work, not to socialize. Luckily, the Baroness was quite comfortable with this crowd. Being her "plus-one" always gave me more freedom to sneak around unnoticed, by most of the guests anyway. The household staff did tend to keep an eye on me, I figured because they were worried I might steal the family silver, given the chance.

Harold adjusted his yellow tie before smoothing down his burgundy suit. Considering he'd built his fortune by importing children's toys, I should have expected him to dress flamboyantly. Yet I couldn't help but cringe at his bright colors and alligator-skin boots, which were better suited for a younger man, instead of our seventy-year-old host. Or, at least, on someone with a less pronounced paunch.

His claim to fame was the "sticky starfish"—a blob of rubber that vaguely resembled a starfish and was coated with a mysterious substance that allowed the arms to momentarily stick to a surface, before slowly crawling down it. He'd hit the jackpot when that blubbery mass became a fad in the early '80s, making him a millionaire in a few months' time. The toy still sold, but not nearly as well as it once had. From my research, it appeared Harold's greatest financial achievement had been reached almost two decades ago, and ever since, he'd spent his life dabbling in one business venture after the other, though none saw as much success as his starfish.

"It is a wonderful twist of fate. Collections such as yours are rare, and many collectors shy away from publicity. I know my magazine's readers will devour this feature on your illuminated manuscripts. Though it is too bad about the auction. I would have loved to have reported on the sale. Speaking of which, there are more people present at this viewing than I had expected, considering you've called it off," I added, hoping to find out why our host had suddenly canceled the sale of fifteen of his medieval prayer books at the last minute.

"Unfortunately, several guests were in transit when the decision was made, which is why we decided to go ahead with the dinner party and private viewing, as we originally planned. However, I am not disappointed that you came, even if your friend, Lady Sophie, will not be able to acquire any of my manuscripts, as she had hoped. Talking with you about my prayer books this past week has been intellectually stimulating. I don't get that chance often because my family has never shown any interest in them."

I smiled modestly, signaling that I'd noticed his compliment, and waved his remark away. "The Baroness, I mean Lady Sophie, will get over it. She has a long list of private auctions she wants to attend during our trip around Europe, which is why my editor wants me to tag along on her buying spree. But my readers would still love to know more about your collection of prayer books—especially now that they will be remaining in private hands. The auction catalogue offers a tantalizing peek, and I bet an exclusive interview with you about a few of your favorites would fly off the shelves."

"Are you certain? I didn't think the general public would be all that interested in them," Harold said with a slight frown, indicating that his ego needed another stroke.

"Of course the readers of *Hidden Treasures* will be interested! Especially since you possess one of the largest private collections of illuminated manuscripts in Europe."

"Actually, mine is now the largest private collection outside of the United Kingdom, thanks to my latest acquisition," he sniffed.

Gotcha, I thought. My hand flew to my chest as I feigned astonishment. "Do you mean the Avron Book of Hours? I had no idea that it put you over the top. My editor is going to be ecstatic when she hears that. Are you still willing to grant me an exclusive peek at the manuscript?"

Harold's chest puffed up with pride. "Most certainly. In fact, why don't we retire to the library now so you can see the books and we can talk undisturbed, before I invite the others in. The way some of the guests are clamoring to see the manuscripts, I doubt I'll have another chance to speak privately with you tonight."

My smile increased tenfold as I dropped my wine glass on the nearest table, then hooked my arm through his. "Fantastic—lead the way."

He grinned at all those present while navigating us across the expansive living room, towards a wide opening that led out into the hallway. As we made our way across the floor, a middle-aged man with black hair slicked back over his rather large head grabbed Harold's arm. He had his mobile phone in his hand and turned the screen towards our host once he had Harold's attention.

"They've closed the train stations, and several roads are inaccessible! How am I to get home?"

"Is the storm that bad, Jacques?" Harold asked with a laugh, his forced joviality betraying his lack of concern.

I looked out the windows wrapping around the concrete and glass structure Harold called home. Rain pounded against the windows, driven by gale-force winds that were effortlessly snapping off branches of the many trees lining the long driveway. Second later, a crack of lightning lit up the skies, revealing angry clouds twisted in shades of gray, followed immediately by an explosion of thunder. The lights flickered momentarily, causing the guests to collectively gaze up at the Louis XIV chandeliers hanging from the ceiling, watching in hushed silence until the tiny electric candles on the many golden arms began to burn brightly again.

Worry crossed Harold's face only briefly. "We've got plenty of space. That's the advantage of owning such a large home," he said as he slapped Jacques on the back. "It's the weekend, enjoy the free food and drink. I'll have the maid make up a room for you."

"I told you before I came down that I didn't want to spend the night! I have an appointment in the morning that I cannot miss."

"I can't control the weather, my friend. Even I'm not that powerful."

Irritation crept into Jacques's voice. "I still do not understand why this could not have waited until Monday."

Harold's eyes narrowed slightly, before he smiled cheerfully again. "It's all about the timing. I promised one of the guests a copy of the documents, but I needed you to sign off first, didn't I? Monday would have been too late. I do appreciate you coming to my home to deal with this business on such short notice."

The man ran a hand over his heavily gelled hair. "Could you at least call the station and see if the trains are running? Perhaps the news report was incorrect."

Harold made a point of staring out the windows long enough for Jacques and I to turn and do the same. "I'll ask my butler to make the call, but it sure looks like you are here for the night."

Jacques's anxious expression didn't lessen, but Harold propelled me forward, regardless. We made it a few more feet before another, even more sullen, guest stepped in front of him, halting our progress once again.

"Dad, do you have a minute?" The willowy woman moved in close and bent her head down to whisper into Harold's ear. Her hair was twisted into an intricate French braid-bun combination that I would never have been able to fashion my unruly hair into—at least, not on my own. I could tell her dress was *haute couture*, but had never seen anyone look so cheap in something so expensive. The glittery black dress was cut in a way that it appeared to be several sizes too large for the thin young woman and hung around her like a potato sack. When she moved, her dress caught the light in the chandeliers, turning her into a rectangular disco ball. Her Valentino slingbacks were also ridiculously expensive, but were not the right pumps for that dress.

Moments after their whispered conversation began, Harold's head jerked back as if she had slapped him. "Raven, you may be my daughter, but you are approaching me as an investor. I meant what I said earlier—I cannot invest in your company right now."

"How can you say that? A month ago, you did believe in what we were doing. What's changed?" Raven pleaded with her voice and eyes.

Her father shook his head and hissed, "This is not the time nor place. I already explained why. It's not my fault you refuse to accept my answer. So let me be quite blunt about it—there is nothing you can do or say to change my mind."

"But other investors are pulling out too because of your decision. Can you at least talk to George and reassure him that my company is solid? He's been avoiding me all night. A word from you might change his mind."

"It's his money, he can do what he wants with it."

"You don't understand—it's your fault George and the others backed out!"

"Enough, Raven, I have a date with a journalist right now. If you will excuse me."

When she opened her mouth to continue, Harold held up a hand, stopping his daughter from speaking further before pulling on my arm, forcing me to tag along.

I looked back to see Raven rooted to the spot, still staring in disbelief at her father.

As we approached the opening from the living room to the hall, I tried to catch my partner's eye, but the Baroness was deep in conversation with the museum curator, Billy Sanders. The middle-aged man twirled the ends of his ridiculously long handlebar mustache in his fingertips as he jabbered away.

The talkative American had flown over from Boston last night, meaning he was already in transit when Harold called off the auction. I assumed he was here to bid on one of the manuscripts for his employer, making this trip a waste of time. At least he would get a vacation out of it.

The Baroness and I had been halfway across France when we received the news and could have easily turned around and headed back to Paris. Yet we'd continued on, in the hope that Harold would allow us into his home. We couldn't pass up this unique opportunity to see the Avron manuscript up close, and hopefully confirm or deny that it was the same book Rosewood sought.

Harold and I had almost reached the hallway, when a Betty White lookalike stepped in our way. "Harold, dear, this has been a lovely evening, but Gary and I really should retire for the evening. Could your butler show us to our rooms? This fantastic home of yours is quite a maze."

Harold released my elbow and grabbed the older lady's hand before gently kissing it. When he raised her hand to his mouth, the jangle of her many bracelets rushing down her arm sounded like a waterfall. Her skin was so transparent, I could see the blood pumping through her veins.

"Belinda, darling, you must stay downstairs, at least for a few more minutes. I have a wonderful announcement to share with you all, but I must speak with this journalist first. Could you grace us with your presence for another half hour? I promise not to dally."

The elderly woman regarded him with watery eyes, before her wrinkled face broke into a wide grin. "Another surprise! Oh my, you are full of them this weekend. Certainly, we will stay. We are deeply indebted to you for opening up your home to us this weekend. Right, Gary?"

She turned to her husband, an even older man sporting a jet-black wig fashioned into a pompadour. He did look quite suave in his velvet waistcoat and charcoal gray suit.

"Quite right," Gary agreed, although by the way he craned his neck around to get a look at Harold, I doubted he had been keeping up with the conversation.

Once we were out of their earshot, I dared to ask, "Would you consider sharing your announcement with me before you tell the others?"

Harold's smile turned mischievous. "It will be more interesting to tell everyone at once. However, I can tell you it is the reason why I agreed to this interview."

"Color me intrigued."

We walked past the stairs, dining room, and kitchen until we reached the other end of the hallway where the library was, its double glass doors closed and locked. A few feet away on my right was one more door, also closed.

Harold pulled out a key and jiggled the door open. "I trust those I've invited, but considering how much my collection is worth and how far off the beaten path our home is, my insurance provider insists I keep it locked whenever my family or I am not inside."

The room was quite spacious, as all the rooms in this house seemed to be. Shelves lined most of the walls, covering them in a quilt of hardbacks in many colors. Five freestanding bookshelves were placed in such a way as to create reading nooks, complete with cushy reading chairs and round tables topped with Tiffany lamps. I ran my hand over a chair's back, reveling in its velvety texture, thinking how heavenly it would be to sit in one of those cozy spaces and read all day.

The two freestanding bookcases at the back of the room were positioned so that they blocked our view of the far wall. Only when we approached did a small opening between the two cases become visible.

The furnishings in this space were even more luxurious than the rest. Two tufted chairs in forest green stood on either side of a nineteenth-century mahogany table topped in blue marble that I estimated to be worth thirty thousand dollars. Lined up against the back wall were five glass-enclosed display cases, tiny spotlights softly illuminating the twenty prayer books Harold was so proud of.

I took my SLR camera out of my purse and held it up to my host. "May I take a few pictures of your library? The space is amazing." I could just as easily have used my iPhone to snap a few shots, but the bulky presence of the large camera body and lens always made a more professional impression on a potential target.

Harold nodded in approval as I made a point of adjusting the lens and crouching down to get a better angle before snapping a few shots of the space.

When I rose, Harold beckoned for me to join him where he stood, in front of the display cases. As I approached, he flipped a switch on the wall and a multitude of lamps lit up the books inside. The glorious silver and gold paints covering the pages shimmered in the bright light. All twenty books were open, revealing a thick Gothic black script on one side and a magnificently rendered biblical scene on the other. These handwritten books contained prayers to be recited daily, the religious text surrounded by a border of lushly illustrated foliage and stylized vines. Accompanying each prayer was a religious scene depicting scenes from the life of Christ or the favorite saints of the benefactor paying for the volume.

Before coming to Villa Saint Marie, I had known that they were important religious documents, as well as miniature works of art. Yet, I still found myself taken aback by their beauty and artistic mastery. The reds, yellows, and blues were so vibrant, it almost looked like they'd been painted weeks ago, not several centuries earlier. The detail in the faces, scenery, and clothing—especially on such a small scale—was exquisite. The artist's mastery with a brush was obvious, even from a distance. I could imagine that with a magnifying glass, one could see the multitude of tiny brush strokes used to create the intricate scenes. Even for someone with little interest in religious art, these were cultural treasures to be cherished.

"Aren't they magnificent?" he crooned. "These prayer books are so delicate, I had these climate-controlled cases especially built for them."

"They are truly breathtaking. Your books of hours will definitely appeal to our readers. I'm going to need to take several photos of those for the feature article."

I noticed that Harold puffed up with pride at my mention of his upcoming media spotlight. *That was easy.* It usually took more conniving and deception to get close to my target. In Harold's case, flattery was all I needed.

After snapping several shots of the open books through the glass, I laid my camera down on the table before taking my notebook and pen out of my purse. Under Harold's watchful eye, I put my nose close to the glass and examined several of the open pages while jotting down the books' names, printed on tiny labels propped up in front of each volume. We moved in tandem along the display cases, towards my target. When I had reached it, I stopped and stared, as if awestruck by the prayer book's beauty. Not that I was faking it—the illustrations were glorious.

"The Avron Book of Hours is the manuscript that put you over the top, isn't it? Could I see it, up close?"

"Why not?" Harold lifted the glass lid and began to reach for the book, when he stopped and turned towards me, a twinkle in his eye.

I had to pinch myself to stop my eyes from rolling, certain he was about to pose another question.

"What do you know about my latest acquisition's creators?"

More than you, I thought. Harold had been testing my knowledge of illuminated manuscripts, ever since I requested an interview with him for *Hidden Treasures* magazine. Although art history is my specialty, I am more partial to paintings and furniture—not rare books. Before I came here, my knowledge of illuminated manuscripts was restricted to the thin file my boss had provided me with, a few reference books I had lying around the house, and a bit of googling. Thankfully, it was obvious from our email exchanges that Harold didn't really know much about medieval prayer books, either.

"In the fifteenth century, the monks of the Avron Monastery created several prayer books for wealthy local patrons and royalty. Only seven copies survive, and all are considered to be the best examples of illustration techniques used in Brittany—and, some say, all of northern France. Because they were handmade, each one contains slightly different illustrations, which give researchers a clue as to which saints the patron found to be important."

What I didn't tell Harold was that one of these precious books had been stolen ten years earlier, and the only way to tell it apart from the others was the presence of a lion wearing a crown that had been worked into the flowering vines filling the title page. It was the only one of the surviving seven to portray that beast on that page. Until I could see it, I could not be certain that the book Harold had purchased a few weeks ago was the same one I sought.

Harold grinned up at me, signaling that I had passed another test. "Well done."

He began to reach for the book again when he suddenly stopped and felt around the inside of the case, instead.

"Almost forgot," he mumbled as he picked up a pair of rather dirty looking cotton gloves. I cringed inwardly, wanting to correct this outdated way of handling ancient manuscripts. Contrary to popular opinion and a plethora of television shows, clean, dry hands were the best way to handle old paper and vellum—not white, cotton gloves. The skin's natural oils helped to keep the pages supple, and bare fingers were more dexterous than gloved ones, thereby making it easier to turn pages without ripping them.

If anything, his actions reinforced my feeling that Harold knew nothing about the million-dollar prayer books in his possession. However, after a split second of indecision, I decided keeping him on my side was more important than teaching him a lesson in basic collection maintenance.

Once both gloves were on, he picked up the book and gently removed it from the case. It fit perfectly into his hand. When he turned around so I could see the jewel-encrusted cover, he announced, as if he were on stage, "Tada—the Avron Book of Hours."

I took a moment to regard the cover: a miniature work of art in silver, with small red and green stones encircling a single large red one as big as a robin's egg. Based on the way the stones reflected in the light, I guessed them to be rubies and emeralds. It was no wonder these books were often worth hundreds of thousands of dollars, if not millions.

"It is beautiful," I breathed, not lying, before grabbing my camera off of the reading table. "You are quite lucky to have gotten your hands on one of these. The Avron books are quite rare, and of the seven copies left in circulation, four are in public museums. It really is a gem."

Harold bowed slightly. "Coming from a fellow art lover, such as yourself, I regard that as a real compliment."

I smiled generously, mentally willing him to show me the title page.

As if he had heard my mental plea, Harold slowly opened the book. It took all of my training not to jump up and down in joy as I gazed upon the title page. The crowned lion said it all—Harold had a stolen book in his hands.

My first assignment back after a three-year hiatus, and after only a week of prep time, I'd managed to find and verify the book as the one Rosewood sought. Best of all, I had done so without having to circumvent an alarm system, disable any bodyguards, or break out my line gun.

I snapped several photos of the title page before he could turn it. With these photographs in hand, the Rosewood Agency's lawyers would have a much easier time negotiating with Harold for the book's return. At the very least, he couldn't pretend that he didn't have it.

I oohed and aahed while he slowly flipped through the rest of the book. "This is one of the five books you were planning to keep, isn't it?"

A dark cloud momentarily passed over Harold's face. "True, there were a few I wasn't ready to part with. But I had not yet acquired this one when I announced the auction, so it couldn't have been part of the originally planned sale. Not that I would want to sell it, or any of the books for that matter—not now."

My mouth pressed into a thin line as I cocked my head at Harold. "Yet three months ago, you announced that you would be auctioning off fifteen of your illustrious books of hours. Why did you change your mind?" I gave him my best "you can trust me" expression.

He gazed down at me as if I had asked something incredibly stupid.

I held my breath, worried I had pushed my luck too far.

After a long and uncomfortable silence, he finally nodded to the Avron manuscript in his hand. "It was only after I purchased this book that the auction house representative told me its acquisition made me the owner of the largest collection of medieval prayer books outside of the United Kingdom. Apparently the previous record holder died a few months earlier and his heirs had sold off his collection, piece by piece. They destroyed its value by doing so, something I want to prevent at all costs."

He stroked the book's cover with his gloved hand. "If I sold those books, I wouldn't have the largest collection anymore, would I?" he said matter-of-factly.

"Makes sense." I nodded vigorously, even though my respect for Harold had vanished in an instant.

There are three types of collectors, in my experience: those who buy art and antiques because they are passionate about them, those who buy as an investment, and those who are driven to possess the most of a single artist or style simply because they are able to. Those were the worst kind of collector—typically completely irrational and likely to send the object underground rather than part with it.

Harold was firmly in the third category.

Seeing as my job permitted the recovery of an object only if I was convinced the owner would destroy or hide it before Rosewood's lawyers could get involved, I pushed for more information. Taking something was always a last-resort measure, mostly because I was not a police officer and thus not really allowed to remove objects from another's home without their permission. When I did it, it was technically stealing.

Yet, as a senior agent for the Rosewood Agency, I was expected to make a split-second decision, and my gut was telling me that Harold wasn't going to give up the book without a fight. Would he burn it or make it disappear? I suspected the latter.

"Aren't you ever worried that you might have purchased something that was once stolen? Or that one of your books is a subject of a restitution case? What would you do if confronted with either dilemma?"

"That's rather dark," Harold laughed, though not as heartily as before. "I only buy from renowned auction houses and expect them to check a book's provenance before they offer it for sale. That's why I pay them an exorbitant commission."

How little he knows about how the art world really works, I thought. His vague and haughty tone had confirmed my suspicions. Luckily he was not a big man, so I didn't expect disabling him to present much of a challenge.

I nodded in understanding and crossed my legs, kicking my heel hard against the chair leg as I did.

"What was that?" I asked, looking behind me with the most frantic expression I could muster.

"I don't know." Harold's forehead creased as he rose and stepped carefully towards the door as if a ninja stood in waiting. Chivalry was not dead, after all.

His movements gave me a moment to prepare. I kept my eye on Harold as I lay my notebook and camera down on the reading table, leaving my hands free to open my purse. Soon my fingers wrapped around the object of my desire.

"Careful," I whispered before standing close behind him and grabbing ahold of his arm, as if I was frightened.

When he looked back to reassure me, I aimed the small bottle of chloroform and sprayed it directly into his mouth.

I supported his elbow as he sank to the floor, then dragged him over to one of the chairs and propped him up in it. It'd been a few years since I'd had to move a body, and my muscles burned, so much so that I had to pause to regain my breath. As soon as I was feeling fit again, I checked that Harold was unconscious but still breathing. Then I pulled a spandex sock out of my purse and stretched it over the Avron Book of Hours. The tight fabric should ensure that the many jewels did not shake loose from the cover during transport.

Once it was wrapped up as snug as a bug, I pushed the contents of my purse to one side, to make room for its bulk. My suitcase had a secret compartment that would perfectly hide something of this format. I wouldn't want to risk flying home with it, but the book should be hidden well enough to get it to the closest embassy without any local cops stumbling upon it.

Before I could get it into my bag, a cracking noise made me turn. The volumes on the upper shelf of the bookcase behind me seemed to be trembling. Come to think of it, the entire bookshelf seemed to be rocking back and forth, as if an earthquake was shaking just that one case. I studied the odd movement, my mind racing through the possible causes. Before I could come up with the answer, I saw a flash of skin and hands pulling back from the now bucking bookshelf, just as a loud groan filled the room and my soul with terror.

The thick wooden shelves had lost their fight with gravity and were racing towards the floor at warp speed. I dived to one side, out of the way of the planks, but couldn't escape the multitude of heavy books raining down on me.

The last thing I remembered was a hardback edition of *Hamlet* plummeting towards my face. Then, everything went black.

10

Smoking in the Rain

The shrill squeal of an alarm pierced through my nightmare, waking me with a start. My heart pounded as the image of *Hamlet* hurtling towards me lingered in my subconscious.

The Baroness sat up in bed, her eye shade already on her forehead. "What's happening?"

"I think that's the house alarm. You stay here, I'll check it out." I grabbed a bathrobe and pulled it over my flannel pajamas before scurrying out into the hallway. Several other guests were already out and leaning over the railing.

"What's going on?" I asked with a yawn.

"Someone set off the alarm."

"I bet it was the murderer trying to get away," another guest cried out, joy in their voice, as they skipped down the stairs. I followed the rest down to the entrance to see what all the commotion was about.

When I reached the ground floor, Tammy was scolding a man dressed in a long double-breasted jacket with a carry-on-sized suitcase by his feet. It was the French guest who had voiced concern about being trapped here for the night. He stood just outside the door and under the covered veranda, yet his jacket and suitcase were already covered in a sheen of rain.

"Where do you think you are going?" Tammy tapped her manicured nails against the doorframe. The ticking noise of the acrylic hitting metal was somehow audible above the shrill alarm, and the combination of high-pitched noises was making me batty.

"I wasn't leaving—I just wanted to have a cigarette," the man stated, as if it was a fact.

Tammy raised an eyebrow. "Really? Do you always take your luggage with you when you pop out for a smoke? Besides, earlier tonight you didn't have any problem lighting up inside of the house."

"Why is the alarm on?" Roger raised his voice to be heard.

"The police want us to all remain inside until they arrive. Jack here knew that because I announced that the alarm would stay on, at the cop's request. You hadn't arrived yet, honey."

Roger crossed over to the alarm pad and pushed in a code, silencing the shrill beeping. "Okay, the show is over, folks. Why don't we all go back up to our rooms. There's still a chance of catching a few more hours of sleep before the day must begin."

The Baroness and I followed the rest back up to the top floor and were soon snuggled back in bed and fast asleep.

11

Forgiving Too Late

The flutter of wings against my window woke me with a start. I sprung up and pulled back the shade to see two robins fighting over a berry-filled branch close to my room. The curtain's movement scared them off, revealing a perfectly blue sky.

I looked out across the manicured French gardens that surrounded Harold's estate, gasping at the extent of the storm damage. It was a shame to see several of the ancient topiaries and pergolas had toppled, taken down by either the wind or falling branches. The grass was hardly visible under the layer of leaves and broken tree limbs littering the lawn. The row of majestic chestnut trees that had lined the two-mile-long drive upon our arrival was no more. Several had been uprooted, their ancient root systems torn out of the earth and now blocking any car's path.

My heart sank a little as I realized we weren't going to be leaving anytime soon, and the police didn't have much of a chance of getting here, either. If this was how our host's yard looked, I could only imagine how badly damaged the country roads connecting this house to civilization were. The only consolation was that the station was close by and we could walk the distance, once the trains were running again.

I tried to keep focusing on the positive: that the storm damage would give us more time to look for the book. If we managed to find the Avron manuscript before the police arrived, that would save Rosewood's lawyers a heap of work and prove to my boss Reggie that I was still qualified to do the job.

The alarm clock began to beep, alerting me to the time. I slapped it out and stretched my arms above my head, yawning until my jaw hurt. My partner was still snoring softly, oblivious to the alarm and the daylight streaming in.

I grabbed my phone and saw a new email had arrived in the night. Myrtle, who was on the West Coast and currently nine hours behind me, had already responded to my update. Her brief message had the same irritatingly motherly tone that I recalled from our previous exchanges.

"Without photographic proof, it's your word against theirs. The family can deny it is the stolen book and easily ensure it would never see daylight again. You should know that! Without hard evidence, we cannot act. So get on it!"

I sighed, knowing she was probably right. Without documentation, Rosewood's lawyers had no real leverage over Harold's family. His being dead didn't simplify things. Until I could find the Avron prayer book again, my assignment was not really complete.

I began to dress for the day, even more eager to search the library after reading Myrtle's message, when I recalled the Baroness's enthusiasm for joining me. I couldn't leave her behind, no matter how much she needed her beauty sleep. After a few tries, I successfully roused my partner, and we were soon on our way downstairs.

I half-skipped my way to the library, figuring I could jimmy the lock before the Baroness caught up, when I noticed that the door was already open. Someone from Harold's family was apparently inside.

When I pushed the door open, a female voice coming from the back of the space made me freeze. I looked to the Baroness and raised an eyebrow, unsure whether she wanted to join me. She nodded towards the back, signaling that we should move forward. Walking on tippy-toes, we made our way towards the voice.

When I looked around the bookcase at the back of the space, my heart skipped a beat. Raven sat on the floor, her hands wrapped around those of her dead father. She was wearing another baggy black dress that reminded me of a potato sack, albeit a very expensive-looking one. In contrast with last night, she wore very little makeup and her hair was pulled back into a ponytail out of convenience, not fashion. Now that I could see her hands, I noted that her nails had been bitten down to the skin.

Her head whipped around, as if she sensed our presence, and she gasped. "What are you doing in here?"

I held up my hands and slowly moved towards her. "Our apologies for disturbing you."

The Baroness stepped forward, as well. "We were walking to the dining room and heard noise, so we decided to take a look."

"Oh." She looked to her father, and her shoulders sagged again. "It was me talking to Dad. We didn't always see eye to eye, but I wanted to let him know that I forgive him for not believing in me."

I leaned back on one heel and regarded the young woman. "Whoa, that's pretty heavy."

"Father and daughter relationships aren't always easy. But that doesn't mean that I didn't love him. Or that I killed him," she rushed to add.

Raven had me there. I never had a father figure around when I was growing up, so I didn't know what kind of complications that could create. "It's a good thing your mother is here to comfort you."

Raven's laugh was low and bitter. "Tammy—comfort me? You have to be joking. She's my stepmom, and we've never gotten along. After I started junior high, my real mother left Harold so she could fulfill her lifelong dream of becoming an airline stewardess, which meant I spent a lot of time at my grandmother's house. Dad met Tammy at some corporate event a few months after the divorce was final. She used to be a bigwig in a marketing company, but after she got pregnant, she married Harold and gave up her career to stay home and raise Roger. I think she's regretted it ever since."

"What makes you say that?"

Raven's chin jutted up in the air. "Tammy's never liked me, but she seems to hate me now that I have a successful business. My accountant forecasts that we will be worth several million once we go public. I have the company and career she always wanted."

"That's admirable," I said, recalling that she and her father had exchanged words about an investment during the party, not long before he was killed. "Is your company still going to go public? It sounded like Harold was taking money out of your company, not investing more into it."

Raven blushed. "Dad was cash poor, that's all. He needed the money for something else, something that couldn't wait, but would have invested in my company again, I'm sure of it. Besides, I know plenty of other venture capitalists that are ready and able to invest in green energy immediately. It's only a matter of time before we're fully funded again."

She looked down at her father's corpse before adding, "When you see Tammy at breakfast, can you tell her that I'll be there in a few minutes. I want a little more time with Dad first."

That was a dismissal if I've ever heard one, I thought. "Of course, we'll be happy to let her know." I nodded to the Baroness and we took our leave.

Frustration rose up within me as a tidal wave about to break. All I wanted to do was find my camera or the Avron book so we could complete this mission and then get out of here, yet I couldn't do so with Raven present. Since I couldn't do either, I decided to distract myself by getting to know the guests better. If I could figure out who took the books, it might help me work out where they had hidden them.

"So much for searching the library. Are you hungry? I could eat a horse."

12

Getting to Know the Suspects

We followed the smell of bacon to the dining room, where a buffet-style breakfast was waiting for us. Sophie and I were the first to partake, and I had to restrain myself from taking more pancakes than I knew I could eat, simply because they smelled so darn good.

The Baroness's apple slices and bowl of yogurt looked lonely on her plate. My breakfast was immense in comparison, but so delicious. And the sheer amount I had taken allowed us to linger longer in the hopes that our fellow guests would tell us something useful.

Even though I still thought Harold's death was an inside job and not the work of a visiting collector, that didn't mean I was correct. In theory, anyone present could have been colluding with either Harold's family or one of the servants.

As the guests trickled in, I made a point of being overly friendly to all of them, asking how they knew Harold and which book they had hoped to bid on. I figured most of them now knew that I was a journalist for *Hidden Treasures* magazine, so I might as well take advantage of the cover and situation.

Only one couple, an investor from Texas and his wife, seemed reluctant to talk to a member of the press about Harold and stayed as far away from me as possible. To my delight, the rest were happy to talk about our dead host, probably because they tried to pump me for more information, as well.

Unfortunately for them, I had nothing new to share. After working the room, it became clear that none of the invitees were friends of his, but American business associates.

"We weren't actually planning on bidding on his books, but it was a great excuse to fly over to see Harold's European digs and take a vacation while we're here," confided one such associate, Belinda, the one who reminded me of the late, great actress Betty White. "The viewing makes it a tax write-off so it's a win-win. After this mess is resolved, we are going to Paris for a week-long shopping spree."

The eighty-plus-year-old was swathed in layers of teal and peach chiffon, and the way her dress was cut, the fabric seemed to billow out around her body whenever she moved. She wore a tiny pendant around her neck, but both wrists were covered with a plethora of thin silver and gold bands. Last night, at the party, she had worn different pieces, but the same amount of jewelry. Considering how much noise her jangling bracelets made, I could cross her off of my list of suspects simply because I would have heard her coming. Whether this rather fragile and elderly woman could have even pushed over the bookshelf was another story.

Another guest leaned over and caught my eye. "Say, you were in there with Harold when he…" The man pretended to gasp before letting his head fall forward as his tongue rolled out of his mouth.

"Nice, George. Real classy," his wife scolded as she slapped him lightly on the shoulder. The couple's nasal accents betrayed their New Jersey roots. He wore a rather boring charcoal-gray suit, but she was exceptionally well-dressed in layers of cotton and silk, with riding boots on her feet and a Hermes scarf around her neck. I always wished I could tie them properly, as she had done.

"Did he show you the Avron prayer book? I always wondered how many illustrations it contained. Harold was bragging about the quality of the drawings, but now that he's gone, Ginger and I won't get the chance to see them up close," George moped before popping a slice of kiwi in his mouth.

"I'm afraid he did not," I lied, not wishing to get into a long conversation with this guy about Harold's collection. My gut told me he was not involved in the theft or murder of our host, but was only interested in gossip. His comment, however, did give me pause.

"Wait a second—I thought the rest of you had seen the books. Tammy mentioned that Harold hung out in the library before dinner so guests could view them at their leisure."

A few others shook their heads, along with George and Ginger. "Most of us missed our chance."

A good-looking man in his mid-fifties raised his hand as if he was back in school. "Julie and I did." Sitting next to him was a gorgeous woman with curly red hair and a well-toned body. She had the age and looks of a typical trophy wife, but not the temperament for the role. Her eyes weren't vacant enough to be a gold-digger—there was too much going on upstairs for her to be nothing more than an accessory.

They were both dressed the part—him in an expensive suit and her in a designer gown that cost more than my monthly mortgage payments. Yet there were still crease marks in his shirt, as if he had unpacked it and thrown it on. I couldn't imagine the Baroness or her snobby friends ever doing such a thing. This crowd was so obsessed with keeping up appearances, they ironed everything—even their bedsheets. Or rather, their housekeepers did. Come to think of it, Julie's dress, in contrast with the rest of the guests, was not tailored to her body, but appeared to be off-the-rack. That was usually a no-no at these kinds of shindigs. I only got away with it because of my cover as a lowly, underpaid reporter.

"Harold even took one of his illuminated manuscripts out of the glass case so we could get a better look at the illustrations. The drawings are pretty darn impressive, but it's the vibrancy of the colors that got to me."

"Me, too," Julie gushed. When she laid a hand over her partner's and smiled, I swore he flinched. "It is as if they were painted last week, even though they are hundreds of years old! You don't get to see that quality of book up close very often, and rarely outside of a museum. Right, Dave?"

"You, bet, hon."

A few guests groaned in frustration, presumably because they had missed their chance to see these valuable and impressive prayer books up close.

Dave took a sip of his coffee and savored it, clearly enjoying the attention, before continuing. As I studied his face, my eyes lingered longer than necessary on his strong jawline and broad cheekbones. Not only was he easy on the eyes, he had a gorgeous head of hair, and a smile that could melt an iceberg. It was too bad he came off as boring and rather irritating during the party last night. From what I could recall, it had felt as if he was interrogating the guests, instead of interacting with them.

"But at some point, Billy came in and started arguing with Harold, something about him reneging on a promise he'd made long ago and that Billy wasn't going to stand for it. When Harold noticed us listening, he rushed Billy over to his office next door. I had the distinct impression that he didn't want us to hear their conversation."

"I think I might know what that was about," Belinda said, as she put a finger to her nose and looked around the room. "Where is our tubby little friend, anyway?"

"I don't think he's come down to breakfast yet," her husband, Gary, answered.

"Billy did have a rough night, by the sound of it," Ginger tittered.

"After Harold rushed off, Tammy asked us to leave the library because she didn't want to sit in there with all those stuffy books, as she put it," Julie, the good-looking man's much younger partner continued, ignoring the comments about Billy. "She said the insurance requires the door to be locked whenever family members are not inside, otherwise they won't pay out in case of a theft."

"That explains why only his family had keys to the library door," I muttered.

"And the housekeeping staff—they have to keep it dusted," Countess Ursula added.

She would know all about running a household full of staff, I thought. "Right, of course, so maybe the butler did it," I joked as I blushed, realizing my mistake in taking Harold's word at face value last night when he said only family had a key. Someone like Harold, who was accustomed to having a full-time staff, wouldn't think to mention that the servants had to be able to get inside to dust, even if he was not home. File that fact away, I told myself before asking

71

aloud, "What were Harold and Billy fighting about?"

"We're not sure," Dave replied. "Billy seemed quite flustered and it sounded like he might have been crying, but Harold got him out of there pretty quickly."

Based on the disappointment in his voice, it sounded like he and Julie had tried to listen in. Who were these two? If they were a couple, they must have recently argued because they were staying way out of each other's personal space. When my husband was alive, I was constantly invading his for a kiss or to simply touch his hand and feel the warmth of his skin.

Before I could push for more information, Belinda leaned over our table to ask Ursula about a mutual friend, one the Baroness also knew. The conversation quickly turned to another exclusive party that several guests had recently attended, and people I did not know. I stood and stretched, while casually looking around to see who else I had not yet spoken to, when I noticed Simone clearing one of the tables. I caught her eye and smiled, hoping she was feeling better today.

She flashed me a grin, but otherwise ignored me. Whether she was embarrassed that a guest was trying to talk to a staff member, or by her show of emotion last night, it didn't really matter. Whatever it was, I respected her enough to leave her be.

When she turned to take the dirty dishes back to the kitchen, an older man making his way to the breakfast buffet slammed into her, knocking the tray out of her hands and onto the floor with a clatter.

"Oh, my! Sorry about that, I didn't see you," exclaimed the guest.

"It's my fault, I should have checked behind me," Simone mumbled before tossing pieces of cutlery onto the tray.

I caught my partner's eye and crossed over to her. "It's as if the staff are invisible," I muttered to the Baroness, who could only shrug.

"Different worlds..." she whispered back.

I shrugged back, knowing she was right. In households such as this one, housekeepers, butlers, and the kitchen staff were meant to be invisible. Considering pretty much everyone in this house had their own household full of servants, they were all accustomed to ignoring the help. My mother's background as a cook in a hotel restaurant ensured that I did notice them, and made certain they knew I appreciated their hard work, too.

As more guests sauntered in, the restlessness in the room seemed to increase tenfold. An older man dressed in orange entered and exclaimed, "Have the police already been here? I heard sirens last night."

His simple question triggered an avalanche of replies.

"That was the house alarm, darling. The police still haven't found time for poor old Harold," Countess Ursula replied.

"Any word on when we can leave this place?" another asked.

"I heard on the radio that several roads along the coast washed out. The trains and buses still aren't running in most of the region."

"Surely the police will make clearing the main roads a priority," another stated, as if he was in a position to know.

I hated this kind of conversation wherein everyone tried to one-up the other with rumors and false information. It was a waste of breath and time.

"Perhaps, but Villa Saint Marie is far from any main road. It may take weeks to get everything cleared."

"Nonsense!" Jacques declared, the desperation in his voice evident. "We can't be expected to stay here for weeks. I'm going to have a word with Tammy as soon as she gets down here. It's her house and thus her responsibility to see that the drive is repaired so that we can leave this place."

"Don't you think she has enough on her mind at the moment?" Ursula replied. "She did say the police would be here as soon as the roads allowed. Harold was murdered and they know that—I should think for that reason alone, making this villa accessible would be a priority."

I turned to regard the speaker. Countess Ursula was the only invitee present who was not family or a former business associate of our now-deceased host. She'd run into Harold at several auctions and they had bonded over their love of rare literature—or, more accurately, their love of the books' value, not their contents.

Her surgically altered face had graced the cover of many an arts and antiques magazine. Her New York penthouse parties were legendary, and the exclusiveness of the guest list ensured they were always front-page news in the society section of *The New Yorker* and *The New York Times*.

According to those same papers, she was anywhere from in her late sixties to her mid-eighties. I couldn't blame the reporters for not being certain. The older woman had clearly had so many facelifts that her skin was pulled as tight as a newly tuned drum. If you squinted or saw her from afar, you would assume she was in her forties, yet her hands were clearly those of someone over seventy. Whoever did the work was good; I saw none of the telltale scars common from extensive cosmetic surgery.

Despite it being early in the morning, her glasses were tinted, making it impossible to see her eyes. The fluorescent green of the frames matched the color of her vintage swing dress. The combination with her candy-pink square heels was enough to get my injured brain throbbing again.

The Countess's key to maintaining her waspish figure was apparently not eating, for all she had picked up from the buffet was a single strip of bacon, an avocado, and a handful of nuts. She gobbled the fruit and almonds up in a heartbeat, but only stared at the sliver of meat. The way she eyed it, I figured the bacon was there to remind her of what food looked and smelled like.

She was clearly the gossip of the bunch and had spent most of the morning flitting around the room, with one hand half-covering her mouth as she whispered delicious tidbits of information into the receiver's ear. I had to assume they were scrumptious, because all of her conversational partners were smiling after their brief chats.

In the Baroness's opinion, the Countess was the worst kind of nouveau riche. She'd been the model hired to pop out of a birthday cake at a charity event her future husband—the late Count Darington—had organized. According to my partner, Ursula had locked onto him from the moment their eyes had met, and within a few weeks she had made the Count her husband, despite their fifty-year age difference. The elderly royal had stayed alive long enough to leave her his title and penthouse; his children got the rest.

Her recent claim to fame was her online video channel. She made a fortune by posting ludicrous YouTube videos poking fun at her New York lifestyle and jetsetter friends. These days, she was one of the wealthiest women in the tri-state area.

From the Baroness's tilted chin and slight crease around her eyes, I could tell she did not like the Countess. However, my partner's negative attitude towards the royal YouTuber may have to do with the social media star noticing that the thick string of pearls the Baroness wore last night was fake. That the Countess openly questioned my partner's jewelry's authenticity was bad enough, but that Ursula found it necessary to make a scene about it, drawing the rest of the guests' attention to the Baroness's faux creation, was enough to start a feud between the two pseudoroyals.

What made things worse was that the Countess was right. The Baroness was certainly wealthy enough to buy real pearls, diamonds, rubies, and emeralds—and did so with gusto. However, ever since one of her jewelry cases had been stolen while she was abroad, Lady Sophie only wore copies of her most expensive pieces—fakes handcrafted to be identical to her renowned and often-photographed necklaces and brooches—while traveling. Bringing the real ones was an insurance nightmare.

Only her tiara, an heirloom that once belonged to the original Baroness Sophie—my partner's great-grandmother—was the real deal. The diamonds in it were plentiful, yet small, and I didn't think it would fetch more than ten grand at auction. However, the sentimental value was enormous, and the reason why Sophie took it with her wherever she went.

Before I could take a seat next to Ursula, the Frenchman who had tried to sneak away in the night entered. I hovered until he had poured himself a cup of coffee, then took a seat across from him.

"Hello, there. Goodness! What an adventure. Did you get any sleep last night, Jack—isn't it?"

The man puffed up his chest. "My name is Jacques, despite what that wench says."

"Oh, so you're not a fan of Tammy."

His eyes narrowed. "Not especially." When he turned away from me and scanned the room, I knew I had to act fast if I wanted answers.

"Why were you so desperate to leave last night?" I batted my eyes and kept my tone light.

He cocked his head at me. "You are reporter, *non?* That is why so many questions?"

"Yes and no. My magazine doesn't cover sordid affairs. I'm just a concerned citizen with a whole lot of natural curiosity. The storm was pretty fierce last night, so I'm trying to figure out why you would want to risk your life by leaving. Unless you had something to do with Harold's murder…"

"*Non!*" Jacques's eyes bulged out of their sockets as he leaned in close, his words leaving a trail of spittle on his cobalt-blue tie. "Do not say such lies! Harold was a business associate, nothing more. I am a notary and helped him with the sale of this home. He knew I was interested in seeing one of his books before it was auctioned off because it reminds me of a volume my mother once owned, so Harold invited me to the party. However, I had no intention of bidding on it, for it is too expensive for me. I was not willing to kill to obtain it, either!"

"That still doesn't answer my question. Why did you try to leave last night?" I kept my tone and gaze as steely as possible. If Jacques jumped up and refused to answer me, then that was it. I had no further recourse, but luckily he did not know that.

Jacques tried to stare me down, but gave up too quickly. His gaze shifted downwards as his tone grew soft. "I am having trouble with the French tax office. It's all a silly misunderstanding, but I am afraid the police may take me into custody if they discover my identity. My lawyer says I have nothing to fear, but I would still rather not get involved with the authorities. I had nothing to do with Harold's death or the missing books, so I had no reason to stay. Whoever killed Harold obviously did so to get the books."

Jacques looked around frantically, as if he was suddenly scared someone had overheard our conversation, before standing up so quickly, the chair behind him tremored. "Now, if you will excuse me…"

13

Roasting the Host

Jacques straightened his tweed waistcoat before stalking off towards another table. Another pair of collectors immediately took his place across from me, loudly offering their condolences before launching into a series of stories about our dead host that did not paint Harold in a positive light. A few others joined in, and soon we were holding our own sort of wake, or more of a roast really.

It was surprising to see that no one really appeared to be bothered by Harold's death. But then again, it didn't seem as if anyone here really knew him well enough to call him a friend.

Other than a few more guests' names for Myrtle to check out, I hadn't learned much new during breakfast. Before I forgot them, I pulled my phone into my lap and quickly punched the names into my phone, figuring I could send them off to Myrtle later.

Which was why I didn't hear Billy enter straight away, but boy did he make his presence known. After filling his plate with a broad selection of sausages, pastries, and waffles, he stood before the rest and gave us his best "how dare you" look. He'd apparently been standing at the buffet long enough to have heard the disparaging remarks about our dead host.

"Have you no respect?" Billy bellowed. "Harold was my friend, and now he's lying dead in the library because someone wanted his things."

"You're one to talk about showing respect. Was that a show tune I heard you singing on your way up to your room last night? Oh, wait, I meant to say, when Roger dragged you up the stairs to your room." George and his wife, Ginger, sniggered as the others joined in.

"Excuse me, do you work for the literature museum in Boston? I love that place," Betty White's lookalike, Belinda, gushed.

Billy straightened up and adjusted his bow tie. "I do. I'm a senior curator there."

She squinted at Billy through her watery eyes. "The last time we visited, that charming new director persuaded us to donate money towards a book they were trying to purchase, the Avron prayer book that Harold ended up buying. That's why we flew over this weekend, so we could see it. Boy, your director was spitting nails about that one."

When Billy began to tremble instead of replying, I interjected myself into the conversation. "Why was the new director so upset?"

Belinda turned to me and smiled. "Apparently one of their curators told Harold about the upcoming sale, and he swept in and outbid the museum. It was quite a painful way for the new director to begin, and he's had trouble gaining support from the local patrons ever since."

"All's fair in love and war, as they say," Billy replied stoically, but I could see his heavily laden plate shaking in his hands.

"Yes, well, the director doesn't seem to trust that staff member any longer. You wouldn't happen to know who he is referring to, do you?" The way Belinda's eyes twinkled, she knew exactly who the director was referring to—and the person in question was standing in front of her.

"No, I do not," Billy protested, but his hands were trembling so badly now, it looked like an earthquake was taking place on his plate. Before Belinda could question him further, he stormed off towards the living room, leaving a trail of eggs and maple syrup as he went.

"Billy's the curator who mucked up the sale, isn't he?" I asked.

Belinda nodded. "According to the director, he is." She dabbed a napkin at her lips and shifted in her chair, as if she was uncomfortable.

I felt like she had more to say, but as a supposed journalist, I was an outsider at these events. Thankfully the Baroness realized I needed her help, for she leaned in and said in a conspiratorial voice, "What else did the director say about Billy?"

Belinda's eyes sparkled as she turned to my partner. "Apparently Harold was too lazy to keep up with upcoming auction sales and relied on Billy to keep him informed. The new director knew that and begged Billy to keep his lips sealed about the Avron auction, but he blabbed to Harold about it anyway. Billy's going to lose his job if he doesn't get the book back."

"Wait—was Billy here for the Avron prayer book? He told me that he was not going to bid on any of the illuminated manuscripts," I interjected.

Belinda tittered. "Honey, his museum doesn't have the money! The donations were contingent on the success of the sale. No Avron book, no money. I bet Billy did steal the books to get it back. Curator positions are hard to come by."

I couldn't help but frown. "He doesn't seem like a killer to me, and murdering someone to keep your job seems pretty extreme."

"You never know what you're capable of until you're pushed. And he would lose his standing in the museum world, as well, if the news about what he'd done spreads further," Gary, Belinda's husband, reasoned.

"So do we think Billy killed Harold?" a guest asked.

"I suppose he could have, but if I had to place bets, I would say that Tammy was our culprit. Did you see how Harold kept running off to chat up that housekeeper last night? I even saw them sneak off into his office before dinner. If I found my husband playing around with the help, I would pack his bags immediately," Ursula said, her tone so bitter and resolute that I wondered whether the topic of infidelity hit too close to home.

When Simone came back into the dining room moments later, Ursula sat up straight and pulled her finger over her lips, making the universal "be quiet" gesture. After Simone cleared up another table and returned to the kitchen, Ursula let out a deep breath as if she'd been holding it in. "That's her!"

"By golly, you're right! I did see them sneaking around and whispering to each other last night. Harold had some nerve, acting like that with Tammy here," another guest exclaimed.

A man in a pinstripe suit joined the conversation. "Harold having an affair with his housekeeper might just account for his strange behavior these past few weeks. We'd been speaking daily about a business venture he'd been interested in investing in, up until recently. During our conversations he'd mentioned several times that he was getting his affairs in order, and then all of sudden, he said he was no longer interested in investing because he needed the cash for something else. Honestly, I got the feeling that he was getting ready to divorce Tammy."

"Oh, speak of the devil!" Belinda tittered.

14

Foxes and Lawyers

At least the pinstriped man had the decency to appear embarrassed when Harold's widow entered. Tammy stopped right in front of the speaker, leaving no doubt that she had heard what was said. "Were you gossiping about me?"

Her tone was as sharp as her acrylic nails. Yet, that seemed to be the only thing on point about Tammy this morning. Her hair, perfectly coifed last night, was now frazzled, her eyes bloodshot, and her makeup even heavier than it had been at the party.

After the pinstriped man shriveled under her gaze, she turned and scanned the crowd, irritation etched on her face. "Where are Billy and my children?"

"Billy is sulking in the living room and your kids are still sleeping, as far as we know," Countess Ursula answered.

"What a bother. Billy!" Tammy shrieked so loudly, I was surprised her dead husband couldn't hear us.

The curator hustled back into the dining room, his plate now empty save for a single croissant. "Yes?"

"Would you join us? I have some news to share with everyone."

"Are the roads open?" Jacques asked.

Tammy rolled her eyes. "Not yet."

"Are you certain?" the Frenchman pushed.

"Yes, I am," Tammy snapped. "The security cameras show downed trees

81

littering the entire drive and blocking the gate. I can only guess how bad the roads are. Besides, everyone has to give their statement to the police before they are allowed to leave. That detective was quite adamant about that, seeing as this is a murder investigation."

"You can't expect us to stay here forever, waiting on the local police to show up. We do have lives, you know," Jacques whined.

"They are going to do their best to send someone over today. Now, can I have everyone's attention..."

Before Tammy could share her announcement, Raven entered and strode over to the breakfast buffet. She poured herself a cup of coffee and leaned against one wall, instead of sitting at a table with the guests.

"Raven, good of you to join us. I have something to share with the group, but before I do, did you borrow my turtle brooch? I can't find it anywhere."

Raven crinkled her nose at her stepmother. "Why would I want to wear something so gaudy? Maybe you overlooked it; you do have a lot of jewelry."

"You know it's my favorite. I wouldn't misplace that one." Tammy snarled, until she noticed the rest were watching with interest. "Never mind, it's not important."

"I wonder if the Silver Fox took it," Belinda said. "Wouldn't that be a horrible coincidence, if he was here at Villa Saint Marie this weekend?"

"Are the police certain it's a man? It could be a really hot chick who's into silver jewelry," a male guest pondered aloud.

"I don't think the police know anything about this Silver Fox, at least not from what I've read about him—or her—online. They haven't a single clue as to who it might be," Countess Ursula shared, her voice a purr.

I cleared my throat, interjecting myself into the conversation. "Pardon my ignorance, but who is the Silver Fox?"

"I thought you were a journalist specializing in arts and antiques. How could you not know about the Silver Fox?" the Countess laughed, gazing upon me as if I was a fool.

As offensively arrogant and derogatory as her comment was, she was right. The past three years, I had done nothing to keep up with developments in the art world—it was all too painful to do so. I made a mental note to check out this Silver Fox later.

"Don't mind Miss Know It All," Belinda said, giving Ursula a sideways glance as she patted my hand. "It's a pseudonym for a jewel thief roaming across Europe. The worldwide pandemic had slowed them down, but now that the borders are open again, they're back out in force. No one knows if it's one person or a gang of thieves, but they are quite adept. Several of my friends have lost necklaces and bracelets to those heathens. They were stolen during parties just like this one, and the authorities still don't know how this thief got in or out of their homes! You would think Interpol would make a priority of it. But then again they're probably too busy attending inter-juridical meetings on tropical islands to actually catch a thief."

Her high-pitched chortle was cut short by Julie, the maybe-trophy wife, slamming her glass down onto a table and muttering something under her breath.

Dave chuckled nervously and patted his partner's hand. "You'll have to forgive Julie. Interpol helped us recover a stolen painting last year, and she's been a staunch defender of them ever since."

Julie tittered as if she was a silly goose, but her smile and laugh were clearly forced. Her supposed husband chuckling along made it even stranger. Interesting. Something felt off about them; I would have to keep an eye on those two.

"Can we focus on the situation at hand?" Belinda cried. "Tammy, was your husband murdered or not?"

Harold's spouse wrung her hands. "I honestly do not know. I tossed and turned about it all night long. The bolts holding the bookcase to the floor appear to have been removed, but until we can clear the entire library, we won't know for certain. They could have popped out and rolled under the other books. However, that still doesn't explain why the bookcase fell over at that precise moment. It's for the police to puzzle out."

She cleared her throat before adding in a loud voice, "While I have your attention, I want to inform you that I am open to bidders on all of the books in Harold's collection—including his illuminated manuscripts."

"Dad's body is still warm and you are selling off his stuff?" Raven cried out as others gasped.

Tammy turned on her stepdaughter, baring her teeth. "He was the one who called off the auction at the last minute, not me! He knew I wanted him to sell off those relics so we could travel the world. That sounds like heaven to me—not being locked up in this stuffy museum in the middle of nowhere!"

Raven glared at Tammy. "Look, why Dad didn't want to travel around Europe with you is your problem. But that doesn't mean you get to peddle off his things, at least not until we are certain they're yours to sell. I don't expect him to leave me much, but we should still talk to the lawyer about all of this before you do anything."

"I've been trying to reach our lawyer since Harold died, but the call won't connect. The cell towers in his region must be down."

"Wait a second, some of the illuminated manuscripts are missing, aren't they?" asked Gary, Belinda's husband. "You can't sell what you don't have—even if you have the right to."

"They can't have gotten far. The alarm has been on all night, which means no one could have gotten in or out without setting it off. I do know that the missing volumes are not under the first editions, as I thought, but they must be somewhere in this house."

Her eyes swept over the group like a search and rescue floodlight. She was all business now, and displayed no sign of grief or sadness. Suddenly her tone turned manic. "Since we're all stuck here, why don't we all try to find them? Think of it as a treasure hunt! Whoever finds the missing illuminated manuscripts gets ten percent off of the valuation price of their favorite one."

Murmurs of interest rose from the small crowd. Considering the missing books were worth a million apiece, the ten percent discount was worth the effort.

"I'll be in Harold's office, in case anyone finds them."

My suspicious mind kicked into overdrive. "Why aren't you helping with the search?"

Tammy pinched her nose as she replied. I wished we could play poker, just so I could take advantage of her tell. "I am aware that until I find Harold's will and can prove his collection is mine, I can't technically sell them to anyone. It must be in his office, but it's going to take a while to sort through the mess he left behind. He threw paperwork into his cabinets willy nilly, instead of organizing them."

Billy the curator sprung up. "Wait a second, if the sale is back on, then my agreement with Harold should be honored, as well. My museum bowed out of five auction sales so that he could sweep in and buy them, without us driving the price further up. He promised to bequeath all five books to us, if we did so."

Tammy stopped and stared at him. "Harold never mentioned this to me."

And that's not what Belinda and Gary said, either, I thought. So were they telling the truth, or was Billy? If Harold was already planning on giving Billy's museum the books, then his director would not have had a valid reason to threaten him with dismissal, would he?

"It's true! A month ago, he emailed to let me know that he wanted to donate the books to us before his death, instead of after. I assumed it was for tax reasons. That's why he flew me over from Boston, so I could pick them up."

Tammy gazed at Billy as if she was seeing him for the first time. "Well, I'll be. Harold never did tell me why those five weren't part of the auction. I wonder if they are the same five that are missing. Wouldn't that be a coincidence?"

By the way she glared at the curator, it was obvious to all that she suspected him of the theft.

He shrunk back from her gaze. "I didn't take them! Why would I? Harold and I had a deal."

"Then why did I see you two quarreling before dinner?"

The museum curator's head shook as he began to sputter a response.

Tammy held up a hand, stopping him short. "Whatever agreement you made with Harold died with him. The new set price is whatever the market will bear. Your museum had better line up a few more sponsors if you want to acquire any of the manuscripts. Around-the-world tickets are pretty pricey."

Billy grew red in the face. "Wait a second—I bet he bequeathed them to us. You shouldn't be able to sell any of his books until the will has been read. I demand you contact Harold's lawyer right now. He can read it to us over the phone."

"Like I said, his phone is not working. Besides, finding the will is only a technicality; I already know who inherits everything—me! Unless you have a notarized copy of your agreement with Harold, don't expect me to hand over millions of dollars' worth of rare manuscripts to your museum."

"That's not right!" Billy stomped his feet, apparently channeling his inner child.

Tammy bore down on him. "Do you know what is not right? That my husband is lying dead in our library, probably murdered over some silly book! That's not right, on any level."

She closed her eyes and seemed to take a moment to center herself before they flew open again. In a loud voice, she added, "Whoever finds the books will be substantially rewarded. Good luck."

15

Pros and Cons

Most of the guests rushed out of the dining room as soon as Tammy dismissed us, chatting excitedly as they set off to find the missing books. I shared in their frivolity. Tammy's announcement giving me a green light to tear the house apart was a godsend.

"It's a real treasure hunt, isn't it?" one elderly, bejeweled woman said to another as they turned towards the staircase.

"Too right. I hadn't expected it to be such an exciting weekend. Kudos to our hosts."

"For arranging for a murder and hunt for stolen goods? What is wrong with these people?" I hissed to the Baroness. All she could do was shake her head slightly, reminding me to hold my tongue. I was on her turf now, and she definitely knew better than I how to handle these people.

"Dibs on the library!" Billy cried as he shuffled out the door and down the hall as fast as his stocky body would allow.

Raven mumbled something about breaking the bad news to her employees via FaceTime as she ambled up the stairs. I could imagine that her father's death would come as a shock to those employees who knew her family personally.

I stood up, ready to join in the hunt. "I hope Billy doesn't lock the library door. I still think the missing books are in there."

My partner sipped her coffee before answering. "Do we really need to look for the books? We know exactly where they are—somewhere in this house. Why don't we let the others find them for us?"

My stomach sank with her answer. My sense of accomplishment and self-worth had diminished considerably since reading Myrtle's message, leaving me wondering whether I was the right person for this job, despite the Baroness's reassurances.

I leaned in and whispered softly, "You heard what Myrtle said. We need to either find the book or my camera, and the chances of the latter still being whole are slim to none. Besides, if we find them first, I can slip the Avron prayer book into my suitcase before the police arrive. Then Rosewood's lawyers won't have to get involved in the legal battle over Harold's books."

A dark cloud passed over the Baroness's face. "We really do need to talk about that. There's been a policy shift, you see, and Reggie would prefer we not remove items from a target's home—unless we are certain it will be destroyed before our lawyers can act. Besides, even if we do find the book, the storm makes it impossible for us to leave the house unnoticed. It's better that we pass the book along to the local authorities and leave it at that."

I exhaled loudly, irritated that she was being so vague, and sank back into my seat. "Why exactly? It's not as if I would steal it, instead of turning it over to the good guys."

The Baroness paled considerably before answering in a voice so soft I had to lean in to hear her. "There have been a few incidents since you retired..."

Before she could continue, two of the kitchen staff entered the dining room and began clearing the dishes.

"Let us resume this conversation at a later time, when we have more privacy. Right now, we need to decide what we are going to do—join the others or wait for someone else to find the missing manuscripts."

"I would rather search for the books than sit on my thumbs. Besides, it might look suspicious if we don't even try to find them."

"True, I didn't think of that." Lady Sophie raised her coffee cup to her lips but didn't sip. Rather, she seemed to be contemplating the situation. After what seemed like a lifetime, my partner finally replied.

"If we find the books, their location may provide a clue as to who had taken them, and perhaps also who murdered Harold."

I nodded encouragingly. "Exactly. The faster the police wrap this investigation up, the faster we get out of here, and the more time we have to prepare for our next assignment."

In truth our next job was over a week away, and there was little prep time needed. We knew where the stolen painting was being kept, and I had already worked out how to circumvent the dogs and alarm system guarding the entrance. However, I hadn't been out of the States in three years and was looking forward to doing a little sightseeing and shopping between gigs.

"To be clear, we will not hide the Avron book in our room, but hand it over to Tammy." The Baroness held up a finger and locked eyes with me. "Assuming they are found before the police arrive, I can imagine they will confiscate the five missing books as evidence. That will make it easier for Rosewood to take action."

"Fine by me." I sprung back out of my chair, wanting to get started before my partner changed her mind again. "Shall we join the hunt?"

I downed my coffee as I stood, forgetting that a lady such as Sophie would never do the same. So I sat back down and waited patiently for her to sip at her drink. Well, I say patiently, but in reality it took all of my willpower not to tap my foot in irritation.

After what felt like hours but was probably less than a minute, Lady Sophie lowered her pinky and cup, before dabbing at her lips. "Ready whenever you are."

16

The Hunt Is On

Lady Sophie rose and dusted invisible lint off of her silver flapper-style dress, complete with a low waistline and lots of shimmering fringe. For most, it would be a bold choice for daytime wear. Yet for the Baroness, wearing something so loose and non-constraining was akin to me wearing sweatpants. "I believe you wish to start in the library."

"I do. If I was the thief, I would have hidden the books in plain sight—meaning in amongst the other books on the shelves. Since I had not yet had a chance to check before Tammy came in and shooed me off, I'd like to begin there."

"What about Billy?"

I shrugged. "Hopefully he'll let us search the other shelves, even if we can't get close to the display cases."

"Lead the way."

As we entered the hall, Tammy's voice caused me to look into the living room. "Hey, be careful with that—it's a Tiffany lamp! I didn't give you permission to trash the place."

Our hostess glared at one of the party guests who, while enthusiastically moving a table, had almost knocked an antique lamp with a stained-glass shade onto the floor. Everywhere I looked, there were guests scouring the expansive villa, taking tapestries and art from the walls, moving furniture, and turning drawers upside down in the hopes of finding the missing books.

We continued to the library and found Billy already busy in the back, where the killer bookshelf and display cases were located. I had expected it to be more crowded, figuring most of the guests would have come to the same logical conclusion as I had about the books' location. But he appeared to be alone.

I blinked in surprise when I realized the bookshelf that had felled Harold was now standing in more or less the same place it had been before someone used it to kill our host. Roger and Billy must have righted it last night during the impromptu wake, I guessed, so as to better search for the missing manuscripts.

We tiptoed towards the back, hoping to catch Billy unawares. I silently crossed myself when I saw Harold's corpse, still lying across the broken chair and table. Tammy, Roger, and Billy must have removed the rest of the books still covering him, as well, for now his entire body was visible. He looked so peaceful. If I hadn't known he was dead, I would have assumed he had simply fallen asleep in a strange, planklike position.

Billy was bent over a stack of fallen books, scanning the titles before reshelving them. Rare first editions of classic literature were still strewn over most of the floor, and only the space around Harold's body had been completely cleared.

Hadn't Tammy said she was certain the manuscripts weren't under the fallen books? How could she be so sure, considering the floor was still littered with them, and several volumes deep? Before I could call the Baroness's attention to this detail, Billy turned to shelf another book and finally noticed us standing behind him.

The heavy man's whole body shook in surprise, and the volumes in his hands clattered onto the floor as he gasped.

"Hey, Billy," I said as nonchalantly as I could.

"What are you doing—trying to give me a heart attack?" He clutched at his chest and bent over, as if he was having trouble catching his breath.

"I do apologize for startling you. We were just looking for—"

"Oh, no you don't." He sprung back up and blocked our path with his body and outstretched arms. "This area is mine. I don't care what Tammy says, the manuscripts could still be under this mess. You two can look over there." He pointed to the book-filled walls on the opposite corner of the library. "But if any of the illuminated manuscripts are in here, my museum should get the discount. Not some private collector who is going to throw them into a safe." He glared at the Baroness as he spoke.

Lady Sophie's spine straightened at the insult, and she seemed to grow a foot as she looked down at the curator. "Just a moment. I have loaned millions of dollars' worth of artwork to several American museums, so the works can be shared with the general public. Don't you dare lump all private collectors together."

I stepped in between them, wanting to snuff out any verbal tiff before it could begin. "I'm not just looking for the missing manuscripts. My camera should be back here, I suspect under those books. I had it with me when the bookshelf fell onto Harold and me. There are several photos on it that my magazine wants to use in an upcoming feature about Lady Sophie."

"If I find your camera, I'll let you know." Billy turned his back to us and continued sorting books.

"Okay, thanks." I took another glance around the space, before crossing over to the bookshelves lining the walls on the opposite side of the library.

After we had retreated, I leaned in close to my partner's ear, hoping Billy wouldn't be able to hear us. "Hadn't Tammy said she was certain the missing prayer books were not under the first editions?"

"Yes, she did," the Baroness replied. From her tone, I could tell she caught my drift.

"How could she be so sure? Unless she had found the manuscripts last night, and then moved them somewhere else, before asking everyone to search for them this morning."

"That's rather devious. But why would she send us on a wild goose chase to find them, if she's already hidden them away?"

"That is an excellent question, Baroness."

"So what do you want to do now—keep looking, in case we are wrong and she does not know where they are at? Or give up and ask the kitchen staff to make us mimosas?"

"As tempting as the drink sounds," I said, licking my lips at the thought, "it's a little early for champagne, even if it's diluted with orange juice. And I do think we owe it to our client to keep searching."

"Fair enough."

Since Billy made clear that the back of his library was his domain, the Baroness and I concentrated on the shelves at the front. She started with the bookcase on the right, and I took the left side. I scanned each of the titles and covers of the novels on one shelf, before checking the space behind them. Based on the number of dust bunnies I was finding, it was clear the bookshelves hadn't been cleaned in quite some time. Why did Harold collect these rare editions of classic literature if he wasn't going to care for them properly?

Meanwhile, Tammy was apparently tearing up Harold's office in her own hunt for his last will and testament. Even from within the library, we could hear her swearing as she slammed cabinets and archive drawers open and shut.

At intermittent intervals, Billy's phone let off a series of beeps, each bringing a squeal of frustration from our curator friend. I was tempted to grab his mobile and set it to silent, but that would have been out of character, so I had to ignore it.

The Baroness and I scanned and prodded each shelf in silence, only occasionally coughing up a bit of dust for our efforts. We'd been at it for a good hour, when my partner cleared her throat. "Having any luck?"

I frowned before wiping a first edition of *Huckleberry Finn* clean with the hem of my emerald satin dress, an off-the-rack Stella McCartney creation I'd treated myself to several years earlier. It was one of my favorites because the color matched my eyes perfectly.

"Nope. I've checked this entire wall, and not found a single clue. Based on the amount of dust, I'd say the books on these shelves hadn't been touched in years. It doesn't look like Harold read much."

"Only two more walls to go," the Baroness replied.

I gazed at the next two bookshelves and tried to laugh, but the dust caused me to sneeze, instead.

I had convinced myself that the thief had simply put the rare manuscripts in among the other books. Yet with a few more shelves to go, I didn't hold out much hope that my theory was sound.

Which made the discovery of a single dust-free plank even more satisfying. It was the lowest shelf and in a darkened corner, meaning it would have been easily overlooked. It was perfect, except for the fact that the missing illuminated manuscripts were no longer behind the first editions lining the plank.

I banged my hand against the shelf in frustration, instantly regretting it. That was going to leave a bruise.

This had to be where the books had been hidden, at least temporarily. So when had the thief removed them, and why? Had they assumed the library would be too obvious, or did they hear me telling the Baroness that I suspected they were still in here? And where did our thief hide them this time?

17

A Grieving Son

I crouched down, trying to feel along the back of that low shelf, in case a jewel had fallen off of one of the illuminated manuscripts' covers, when a peal of laughter made me jump.

Standing in the doorway, swathed in a bathrobe with his hair sticking up in spiky tufts, was Harold's son. The groggy-looking young man held a cup of coffee in one hand and a half-eaten croissant in the other.

"You two are being thorough. Lady Sophie, your face is covered in streaks of dust, and you seem to have a few cobwebs in your hair, Carmen."

My partner's eyes widened to saucers as she rubbed at her cheeks and hair. Luckily for the Baroness, she had already removed her trademark tiara, for fear of bumping it against a shelf and damaging it while searching.

"Yes, well, it was all for naught. It appears that someone did hide the books back here, on this low shelf, but moved them," I said, letting frustration infuse my voice.

Roger stiffened. "How can you tell?"

"It was the only one that wasn't covered in dust. The thief made a good choice—it's almost hidden from view so a casual visitor wouldn't have easily stumbled upon it."

Roger nodded in appreciation as he grinned, revealing his pronounced hook teeth. "I'm impressed—you aren't just a pretty face."

Was that supposed to be a compliment or an inappropriate advance? He had to be twenty years younger than me and not at all my type.

"Yeah, there's actually a set of brains in here, not just air." I tapped my skull and laughed, while telling myself to calm down for fear of scaring him away. It turned out, I need not worry.

"Spicy—I like it. Good luck with your treasure hunt."

When he turned to leave, I saw my chance to ask him about the cufflink slip away. So I hustled towards the door to block his path. "I'm sorry about your dad. Were you two close?"

It may have been my imagination, but I swore when Roger looked down at me, his eyes narrowed slightly and his mischievous grin dimmed a few watts. "Close enough. I live in Las Vegas, so we haven't seen each other much since he moved over here. But Mom kept me in the loop."

"Do you work in a casino?" I feigned surprise, curious to see whether he was going to lie about his occupation.

"Sort of. I'm a professional gambler."

"Ah, that's why your watch costs as much as my car," I chuckled, causing Roger to guffaw and the Baroness to wince. "That must be exciting, living the high life."

"It has its moments. Being self-employed does make it easier to fly over to be with Mom when she needs me."

"We are sorry for your loss," the Baroness emphasized. "It must be difficult for you, having flown all this way, only to find out your father had been murdered minutes before you arrived. And now this robbery."

He shrugged and looked to the floor.

"It's good your mom and sister are here with you," I added. Being an only child, I had no personal understanding of the sibling bond, but knew they were supposed to comfort you in a time of need. Which is why his reaction to my comment—a slight frown and stiffening of the spine—surprised me.

"Half sister, but yes, it is." He looked again towards the door and I wondered how much longer he would put up with my questions before excusing himself.

"Not to be rude, but why did you and your half sister come out to the house last night? I thought the party was supposed to be for business associates. I hadn't expected Harold to have invited family." I hoped I wasn't pushing my luck, but something told me this would be the only time I would get to talk candidly with Roger.

"I don't know why Raven flew over, but Mom called me a few days ago and asked me to get over here as soon as I could. Dad had been feeling poorly lately anyway, but the upcoming sale had set him on edge and she was worried the auction would be too much for him. He was quite attached to his collection, and we all knew it had been a difficult decision for him to put them up for sale. So I got a red-eye to Paris and took the train down from there." He looked down at his bathrobe and grinned. "Jet lag's a killer."

I agreed, wishing I could lounge around in a bathrobe, as well. However, I was not able to admit that I was in the same boat, because my cover stated that I'd already been in Europe for three weeks. "It's a good thing you made it down here before the storm hit. Otherwise you probably would have been stranded halfway."

"It didn't make things easier, that's true. But the house is a short walk from the train station and it was easier to dodge the fallen branches on foot."

His comment reminded me of Jacques's concerns about being able to get home the night of the party, and how several roads had closed and the trains had stopped running hours before Roger arrived. Which meant he must have been in the village long before he rang the front doorbell.

The hairs on my neck prickled. Roger was clearly lying, but was he also our killer? Sure, he was arrogant enough that I wouldn't put it past him. But why would he kill his own father? Perhaps his reaction to the cufflink would be a tell-all.

"Hey, while I have you…" I dug around in my purse until my fingers closed over the piece of jewelry I'd found in the library earlier. For safety's sake, I had wrapped it in a tissue. "I believe this is yours."

Roger's eyes lit up as he reached for it. "There it is! Dad surprised me with these cufflinks after I won my first poker tournament. I'd noticed one was missing earlier, and was worried it had gotten snagged on something in the plane and that I'd never find it again." He examined it briefly before pocketing it. "Where did you find it?"

"In the library, close to your dad's body." I nodded my head in the direction of Billy, still busy clearing the floor of fallen hardbacks.

"Oh, it must have dropped off when I helped move the bookcase off of my father's corpse."

Something about his tone made me perceive his words as a threat. Was he trying to get me to leave him alone, or was it simply this entitled young man's manner of speaking? I saw no point in antagonizing him further, so I backed off. "I guess it must have. Again, we are truly sorry for your loss."

When a phone began to ring in his pocket, I started a little at the noise. The bump on my forehead had reduced to the size of a golf ball, but the unexpectedly loud noise still set off a drum solo in my head.

Roger's face drained of color when he looked at the screen. His eyes scanned the room frantically, as if he were searching for a place to hide. "I need to take this."

He answered before he pushed past me and exited the library, speaking rapidly in a low tone. "I'll have it all to you next week. It's become more complicated, but not impossible. I have to talk to my mom about..."

Unfortunately, his voice faded before I could hear the rest. Hearing the arrogant and self-assured Roger pleading and groveling made me realize how much appearances could deceive. I turned to my partner. "Sophie, I think Roger killed his dad."

"Why would he do such a thing?"

"I'm not entirely certain, but I would guess that it has something to do with money. He's lied to us repeatedly since he arrived."

"What do you mean?"

"Well, he said he came down from Paris, but he didn't ring the doorbell until several hours after the trains stopped running. Which means he probably arrived much earlier, giving him time to enter the house undetected, kill his dad, hide the books somewhere in the library, and then go back outside and ring the bell, as if he had just arrived."

My partner looked shocked. "Oh, my. You're right, he has no alibi. I suppose there were enough guests milling about that his presence could have gone unnoticed. But how would he have gotten the books out of the library?

And where did he move them to?"

"About a half hour after he and Tammy put Billy to bed last night, I heard Roger in the hallway again. He was alone that time, but holding a covered silver platter, the kind you use to keep your meal warm. What if it was not food, but the five books under there? Last night, I figured he was hungry because he missed dinner. I didn't suspect him, until now. He could have moved them from the library into his room, and no one would have been the wiser."

"That would explain why we didn't find the missing books in the library, even though it is the most likely hiding place. At least, initially." The Baroness was clearly warming up to the idea. "As well as why Roger wasn't searching for the books."

"And he knows the alarm code," I said under my breath as another recollection filled my brain.

Lady Sophie ticked her tongue against her teeth; she hated it when I muttered. "What did you say?"

I made a point of enunciating my words this time. "When Tammy caught Jacques trying to sneak out of the house, it was Roger who turned off the alarm. I don't recall him asking Tammy for the code—she was too busy interrogating the Frenchman."

"So Roger had the means and opportunity, but that still does not answer the question as to motive. If he is in financial trouble, you would think his father's death would be detrimental."

I cocked my head at her.

"Now he can't ask dear old dad for a loan, but will have to wait for the estate to settle. Harold was the owner of, or major shareholder in, several companies, which will significantly complicate the distribution of wealth. Tammy probably won't have access to any of his savings accounts or investment portfolios until the curator has paid all of his outstanding debts. In situations such as this, it could take months, or even years, before any money is disbursed."

"I didn't think of that..." I mumbled, knowing she was right. If Roger needed cash fast, killing his dad was not the way to go about it. But was stealing his books any better?

"What if Roger stole the manuscripts so that he could sell them, and accidentally killed his father in the process?" my partner asked, as if she was reading my thoughts.

"He could have done so, in the hopes of selling them off to a private party who was willing to be discreet. But the missing bolts and the arms I saw pushing the bookcase over tell me that Harold's death was no accident."

We both sat in silence, contemplating the situation, until another thought struck. "There is still the mystery of the missing bolts, but Tammy's involvement would help clarify their disappearance."

"What do you mean?" the Baroness asked.

"Those bolts holding the bookshelves onto the floor must be quite long if only four of them could hold it in place. It would have taken time to remove them, not to mention have made a lot of noise. Roger wouldn't have been able to do that during the party without someone noticing. But Tammy could have removed the bolts before the party even started and told him which bookcase to push over."

The Baroness gasped as her hand flew to her throat. "Are you suggesting that Tammy and Roger did this together? I've heard of many different plots to kill a loved one for money, but helping your son to murder your husband takes the cake."

"True. But if that lawyer was right, and Harold was getting his affairs in order because he was planning on leaving his wife for Simone, then perhaps Tammy did kill him out of revenge. Or to ensure he didn't write her out of the will."

I turned towards the library door, determined to get to the bottom of this. "So, if we assume Roger pushed over the bookcase, took the illuminated manuscripts out of the display cases, and then moved them to his room last night, that means they should still be up there. We really need to search his bedroom, preferably before someone else thinks to do so."

The Baroness's eyes twinkled. If she hadn't been so well-bred, I bet she'd have clapped her hands together in glee. "Oh goodness, another break-in. How enthralling!"

18

Antiques Time

As we walked down the hallway towards the staircase, a niggling thought made me change direction. "Before we search his room, let's make a quick detour. If Roger really did make himself a meal and take it up to his room last night, the kitchen staff might have seen him. If that platter was hiding a meal, then we are wasting our time. It's a long shot, but might be worth the effort."

I knocked twice before slowly opening the kitchen door, not wanting to bash into a worker in the process. Standing inside were two women, washing several pots and pans by hand.

When we entered, a familiar voice caused me to look to the television mounted in one corner. To my surprise, my best friend was smiling back at me from the small screen.

The two employees stopped washing and looked at us in expectation. I tried tearing my eyes away from the television, but was too shocked by Rhonda's presence to do anything but stare at her.

When neither the Baroness nor I spoke, one asked in lightly accented English, "How can we help you?"

Her question snapped me out of my trance and reminded me of why we were here. "Do you know if Roger ate any dinner last night? He showed up so late, we were concerned about him. He hasn't yet come down for breakfast," I lied, too easily, I'm afraid, hoping they had not seen him grab a cup of coffee. "If he hasn't eaten yet, we thought we might bring some pastries up to his room."

Both women shrugged before the older one answered. "I can't really tell, to be honest. We cooked so much food because of the party, I could not tell you what he took or how much—the refrigerator was full of leftovers."

"Right, that makes sense. Are you missing any dinner trays or platters?"

"Just the one, but Roger has it in his room. Tammy informed us when she came down."

"Oh, okay. Then he must have eaten already. That's a relief—right, Lady Sophie?" I said with a forced smile. So Tammy knew that Roger had taken a tray upstairs, which meant she probably knew what was underneath the cover. I examined the other silver trays. They were large enough to fit two full plates of food under the domed lid, which meant the five books could have fit under there quite easily. So had Roger taken food or the books up to his room?

"Yes, it is. Thank you for your assistance." The Baroness nudged me and nodded at the door.

When I hesitated, my eyes locked on my best friend's face peering back at me from the television, the older worker asked politely, "Is there anything else we can help you with?"

"No," I muttered, trying to stay on track, but the television show distracted me. I pointed to the small screen, upon which my best friend was presenting her show, *Antiques Time with Rhonda Rhodes*. "I'm sorry, I know this program from back home. Is it popular here, too?"

The kitchen staff gazed at the television and then up at me with a puzzled look on their faces. "You mean *Antiques Time*? Yes, we all love to watch it. I just adore Rhonda Rhodes; she is quite the character. The head chef has even started dressing like her when she's off duty."

"You mean with lots of fringe on her sleeves and low-cut blouses," I laughed.

The housekeeper blushed and nodded. "Pink cowboy boots and glittery scarves are now her favorites."

I made a mental note to tell Rhonda, before nodding to the Baroness, signaling that we could leave.

"Thanks for the information and the food. The party was lovely, well, except for the dead guy," I babbled as I followed her back out into the hallway.

When we were alone again, my partner looked at me questioningly. "The show's host did look familiar. Isn't that a friend of yours?"

"It is, and she is going to love knowing her show is a hit in Europe. Let's check Roger's room and see if our theory is correct."

19

Where There Is A Will

We had just started up the staircase when a blood-curdling scream pierced the air, causing us to run instead of walk. It was coming from Harold's office, next to the library.

I sprinted toward the noise, certain someone else was being murdered. Instead, I found Tammy, standing a few feet away from Harold's desk, her face as white as the sheets of paper she was clutching in her hand. The way she held the pages far away from her body, you'd think they were poisonous.

"Harold lied to us, Roger. He cut us out!" Tammy cried.

"What is that?" Roger raced over to his mother and pulled the paper out of her grip. His face also drained of color as he read the three-page document. "Is this a joke? Dad didn't seriously change his will to benefit..." He looked up and searched the room frantically, before screaming as if his life depended on it. "...*Simone?*"

"What is there?" Raven cried as she entered. When her brother showed her the documents, her face fell, as well. "You have got to be kidding me! Tammy—tell me this is some sort of sick joke."

All her stepmother could do was shake her head. "It's right there and in black and white—Harold has already sold his book collection to Roger Wainwright for a royal amount and the proceeds go to Simone. I should have known that sneaky charlatan would get his way, in the end. He'd been after Harold's collection for months." She fell into a wingback chair, seemingly broken emotionally.

I was as shocked as Harold's family was. After that song and dance he spoon-fed me about wanting to keep the collection together, Harold had actually pulled the books out of the auction because someone else had apparently offered him more.

"But how did Simone worm her way into Harold's will?" Raven asked.

"This must be some sort of horrible joke. Those books are the most valuable things that Dad owned," Roger cried as he looked to his mother. "Does Wainwright know the sale benefits Simone and not us? We have to talk sense into him before he transfers any money over to her. He's one of us; he'll listen to you, I bet."

My hackles rose as I took in Roger's words. People like him got away with far more than they should, thanks to their wealth and well-connected friends. It was the Simones in this world who needed protecting from vultures like him.

"I can speak with Wainwright, but it appears your father already signed a contract with him. Harold agreed to loan him the collection now, but the sale only goes through after Harold's death, so that the price can be adjusted with inflation, and the profits are to be transferred into a trust fund in Simone's name. Boy, he sure thought of everything," Tammy said, her voice strangely calm.

Billy stepped forward, his whole body trembling as he asked, "You mean all of the illuminated manuscripts have been sold to Wainwright—except the five he promised my museum, right?" Billy took advantage of the family's collective depression and grabbed the papers from Roger's unresisting hands. Yet his expression only grew paler the further he read.

"I can't believe it; he lied to me. And I thought we were friends." Billy choked back a sob. "Why did Harold tell me he was giving my museum five of his illuminated manuscripts if he had sold them to some private collector? He even bought my airplane ticket over here."

"I don't think he lied when he told you. He changed his mind so suddenly, he must have forgotten to call and let you know," Tammy said, after no one else bothered to reply to the curator. She was taking this life-altering news much better than I would have expected her to. The children, on the other hand, were not ready to accept Harold's most recent decisions without a fight.

Roger grabbed the pages in Billy's hand, but the museum curator was not ready to let them go. "I demand a copy, so I can send it to our lawyer!"

While the two men played tug-of-war with Harold's last will and testament, I leaned over to whisper to my partner. "How could Harold forget to tell Billy he'd sold the books to someone else? You would think he would have been the first person Harold contacted, seeing as Billy was flying over from the States to pick the books up."

"We didn't receive Harold's message until the night before the party, when we were already driving down from Paris," the Baroness reasoned.

"True," I replied softly. "I guess it just proves that Harold really did wait until the last minute to announce his decision."

"Let go!" Roger screamed, the force of his words seeming to scare Billy long enough to let him pull the pages out of the curator's chubby hands. "There's no reason to make a copy of this will because it's not valid. It can't be!"

When Roger turned to his mother and spoke, there were tears in his eyes and his voice softened to that of a little boy. "Why would he do this to us? First he cancels the auction, and now we find out Dad left the bulk of his estate to a stranger. How am I going to pay my debts off now? Mom, can you help me out again?"

Tammy's face paled. "Harold was done bailing you out, and so am I."

Her son's face grew ashen. "But they're going to break my legs!"

All Tammy could do was shake her head. "You stupid little boy. I warned you about borrowing from loan sharks, but you wouldn't listen! I can't help you, even if I wanted to. I don't know what your father was up to, but last month he transferred almost all of the money we had in our bank accounts to a Swiss company—and didn't say a word to me about it! There's barely enough left in our checking account to pay the electricity for the coming month. How do you think that makes me feel, after being married to him for thirty-two years?"

"Can this get any worse?" Raven cried.

Tammy sank further into her wingback chair. "Keep reading, children, it gets much worse."

Raven stood next to her brother and together, they gazed down at the paperwork, their expressions growing more perplexed the longer they read.

While the Moreau family studied Harold's new will, I took in his office. It was a large space, yet in contrast to the rest of the house, it felt sparsely decorated, despite the many filing cabinets lining the walls, and the wide desk spanning one end of the room. The furniture was also different from the rest in that it was banged up and not highly polished. The desk was not a Louis XV-style marquetry desk, as I would have expected given Tammy's other choices, but a nondescript scruffy thing with missing handles and at least one broken drawer.

The two wingback chairs, one currently occupied by Tammy, looked comfortable enough, but their fabric was wearing thin in spots. The table they were placed around, a square piece made of a dark mahogany, was clearly the most expensive thing in the room, yet wasn't worth more than few hundred bucks.

Did Harold not appreciate high-quality furnishings? Or had his office been off-limits to Tammy when she had been hunting for furniture?

Whatever the reason, paperwork now covered the desk, the table, and much of the floor. Based on the many open and empty drawers, I would say it was the contents of two archival cabinets that had been strewn across the spacious room.

Because the family was distracted, I moved closer to Harold's desk to see what I could find. An agenda was open to this week, and two appointments had been scrawled onto yesterday's date: "Jacques—get docs ready!" and "Book Party" with a frowny face drawn next to it. It appeared our host wasn't as excited about the party as he had pretended to be. More intriguing to me was the name Jacques. Was that the same Frenchman who had tried to sneak out of the house last night? I made a mental note to ask him about it, then resumed my visual search.

On the corner closest to me, a flyer for a French realty company aimed at expats caught my eye. I moved it closer, and when I did, the paperwork underneath was revealed. It was a folder for a travel agency. Luckily for me, Roger, Raven, and Tammy were so focused on Harold's will, they didn't seem to notice me snooping. Feeling brazen, I stepped closer to the desk and lifted the folder's edge up enough that I could read the itinerary inside. Someone was heading to Switzerland, but that person was not Tammy.

Before I could slip it off the desk, Roger erupted with such a force, I stepped backwards automatically.

"I don't believe a word of this nonsense. Either Dad had lost his mind, or Simone manipulated him into believing this ridiculous assertion..." Roger's voice trailed off as he stared in disgust at the will.

"We have to find a way to fight this. What if we can show that Simone manipulated Harold into changing his will in her favor? That must be illegal," Raven raged, practically foaming at the mouth.

Roger apparently agreed, for he stormed out into the hallway screaming Simone's name.

The butler poked his head over the railing on the top floor. "Sir?"

"Jeeves—find Simone and tell her to get down here!" Roger shrieked.

A few moments later, the middle-aged housekeeper peeked over the railing, an iPod earbud hanging out of one ear, folded bedsheets in her arms. "What is there?"

"Get down here—now." Roger's demanding tone set my teeth on edge. While most of my targets had a house full of servants doing their cleaning and cooking, my American sensibilities still had trouble with the whole upstairs-downstairs concept.

"Yes?"

When Simone entered, Roger asked in a thunderous voice, "Are you Simone Cherie Duchamp?"

Out of the corner of my eye, I noticed the butler flinch. Considering the man's constant mask of neutrality, the small crack in his armor was quite noticeable. So why would Simone's full name, of all things, cause this consummate professional to slip up and react?

Roger thrust the papers into her face. "Why did my father leave you his entire book collection? I don't buy this nonsense about you being his daughter."

Daughter? My jaw dropped as I took in the scene before me. Roger, Tammy, and Raven stood opposite Simone, glaring at Harold's recently discovered kin.

Simone's shoulders squared as she grabbed the pages. The room was dead quiet as we all waited for her to get through the document. A smile split her face when she reached the end.

"I hadn't expected Papa to be so generous." She emphasized Papa, making Roger cringe visibly.

"How dare you use that word—you imposter! What's your proof?" Tammy roared.

"DNA testing—Harold demanded it. After it came back positive a week ago, he welcomed me with open arms and promised to change his will to include me. I didn't expect him to actually do it, and definitely not so quickly. And now the proceeds from the collection's sale are mine!" Simone giggled.

"Wait a second—did you know that he'd sold his illuminated manuscripts to one collector?"

Simone nodded. "Harold said a man named Wainwright offered to buy the entire collection for double the price he'd been expecting to get via the auction. Last I heard, they'd already drafted the sales agreement, but hadn't finalized the transaction yet."

"This can't be happening!" Tammy wailed. "I know Wainwright has been after his illuminated manuscripts for quite some time, but Harold never mentioned that he'd sold the books to the man, and I am his wife."

"I can't believe Dad already changed his will," Roger grumbled. "He just found out about you being his daughter, and yet he jumped through all these hoops to include you? If you really are his daughter, why did you show up now, instead of when you were eighteen? You've got to be sixty pushing seventy."

Simone straightened up as much as her short frame allowed. "I'm fifty-two, thank you very much. And I only found out about Harold being my dad a few months ago, right before my mother passed away. She didn't include his name on the birth certificate, and she only told me because I begged her not to leave me wondering for the rest of my days."

"So why are you working here as a servant?" Roger crossed his arms across his chest.

Simone's hands flew to her hips. "I am a housekeeper, not a servant. It was the easiest way to be close to him, without alerting the rest of you. I didn't get up the nerve to tell him the truth until a few weeks ago, and that was when he asked me to do a DNA test. Only after it came back positive did he start to open up to me. It's such a shame that we just found each other and now he's gone—we had so much catching up to do." Simone wiped away a tear. "He was going to tell Tammy the truth about me after tonight's party so we could be a real family."

Tammy laughed. "You have got to be joking! You're not one of us and never will be."

Roger pointed an accusatory finger at Simone as his voice rose an octave. "All of this is your fault! You owe me a hundred grand; it's the least you can do."

"You expect me to give you a hundred thousand dollars? Even if I had that kind of money, why would I help you? I have worked my fingers to the bone every day of my life. But you drive around in a Lamborghini and live in a penthouse. Don't try and deny it—I've seen your Facebook page! And is that a vintage Rolex on your wrist? I only recognize it because they are on the news so often. Apparently those kinds of watches are hot targets for thieves, thanks to how much they cost," Simone spat.

"You don't understand." Roger's face flushed. "They are all part of my uniform. Without my watch, car, and clothes, I wouldn't be invited to the high-roller table. Without sitting there, I have no chance at winning enough to pay off my debts."

Simone continued as if Roger had not spoken. "That's why Papa agreed to that interview with *Hidden Treasures*. He wanted the world to know that he had amassed the collection, not Wainwright."

When Simone smiled at me, Tammy exploded. "I don't believe a word you're saying. Why would Harold give a virtual stranger his most precious possessions?"

"It's the truth. I had a rough childhood, and he wanted to make up for not being there to help. He told me that he'd bailed Roger and Raven out enough times already, and they had to learn to stand on their own. Most of all, he felt bad that he wouldn't have time to get to know me better because he was dying..."

Tammy clutched at her throat and began hyperventilating. "He was what?"

Simone cocked her head at Harold's spouse. "He had inoperable prostate cancer and the doctors gave him a few more months to live. That's why he transferred all that money to a Swiss clinic. It was a down payment for the medical treatment he expected to receive, but the handlings would only lessen his pain, not extend his life. Didn't you know?"

"No!" Tammy wailed and fell into her son's arms. Raven's face paled even further before she rushed out of the room.

"None of this is true; it can't be. He wasn't sick, and you aren't his biological daughter." As Tammy pulled back from her son, she seemed to rise in stature, as well. "Until I can talk to a lawyer, I refuse to believe that this will is valid, either."

Tammy turned and raised her voice so as to address the party guests gathered around the open library door. "My offer still stands—these books are going to be sold, and no housekeeper is going to stop me, no matter what this paper says."

Simone leapt in between Tammy and the small crowd. "Don't listen to her—she can't sell what's mine!"

Before Tammy could respond, Simone bent down and picked up a handful of Harold's files.

Tammy sprung up and slapped her hand away. "What do you think you are doing? Those are my husband's private documents!"

She made a move to open another drawer when Tammy blocked her way. At least, she tried to. The housekeeper shoved Tammy aside and reached for another pile.

"The titles for the illuminated manuscripts must be in here somewhere. Harold said his buyer was sending a representative to arrange the transportation, and I want to find them before you can do anything dastardly with them," Simone said as she dug further into the file cabinet.

Roger pulled Tammy up to her feet as she screamed, "If Wainwright dares to send one of his men here, he'll have to go through me to get to them. So do take your hands off of my husband's things and get back to work."

Simone tore off her apron and threw it down at Tammy's feet. "I'm not your maid anymore! As their rightful owner, I demand you hand over the titles to the illuminated manuscripts."

"I will do nothing of the kind! Now get out of my house!" Tammy fired back.

I leaned over to my partner. "This is going nowhere fast."

20

Social Graces

When Simone began throwing verbal slurs at Harold's wife, I touched the Baroness's elbow and nodded towards the door. It was clear that this squabble was only going to intensify, and the ensuring cat fight was neither any of my business nor helpful in my search for the missing collection. It would, however, keep the pair out of our hair for a while.

Once we were out of earshot, the Baroness whispered, "I can hardly believe that Harold changed his will so suddenly, and in favor of a person he barely knew. Poor Tammy. You may not like her, but that's got to be quite a shock finding out your husband had a secret child and also left it the bulk of his estate. They have been married for more than thirty years."

My irritation with the new widow dissipated a little in light of Sophie's comment. "You're right—that had to be a huge shock for Tammy and Harold's other kids. Yet I suppose it's not too surprising that he made such a drastic decision without telling them. From what everyone has said about our late host, it seems that Harold was quite unpredictable."

I headed towards the staircase, hoping to search Roger's room before the fight broke up. However, when I spotted Raven hunched over on a couch in the living room, her whole body trembling, I presumed, because of grief, I couldn't help but change direction. Out of the corner of my eye, I could see the Baroness trail after me, albeit somewhat slowly.

"Hey, Raven, are you alright?"

It was a stupid question and a waste of breath, I knew, but socially acceptable and even expected at a time like this. Besides, I knew my partner wasn't going to jump in and take over.

"No, I am not alright!" Raven exploded. "I am furious with my father. He cared more about a servant he'd only just met than his own flesh and blood."

"Technically, she is also his flesh and blood, as you call it…" I said, then let my voice trail off when she glared at me.

"You don't understand—it's not as if he was there for me when I was a kid. So why does she need to be made up to? What about me?"

Her answer caught me off guard. "I thought you lived with him growing up."

"Nope. He despised my mom for leaving him and didn't fight for custody. I only saw him for a week during my summer vacations, and he always seemed more interested in finding out who my mother was sleeping with than in spending time with me. I resented him for that. I was fifteen when Roger was born, and after that, I hardly ever saw him—Harold said he was too busy to care for two kids. What he really meant was that he was too busy to care *about* two kids."

"Okay, so you two were estranged. I can see why you were upset with him."

Raven snorted. "Estranged is putting it lightly. Harold was a horrible father. It's not fair that Simone didn't have to suffer any of his pain, but gets the bulk of his estate."

Before I could think of something comforting to say to this virtual stranger, Raven sat up straight and wiped at the tears running down her cheeks, as if she was suddenly embarrassed by them. "Who am I kidding—it's the same old story, isn't it? Dad was obsessed with his work and spending time with his family wasn't a priority. Didn't Cat Stevens write a song about that?"

"*Cat's Cradle*—I know that song well." In contrast to most listeners, I always wished I'd at least had what Cat Stevens described in that song. I would have given anything to have had a father who was too busy to spend time with me, rather than not having one at all.

"I thought we'd finally reached a turning point in our relationship when he started taking an interest in my company. He offered to invest in it—I didn't ask him to, despite what Tammy has told everyone. Which is why his sudden decision to backtrack on the capital injection he'd already promised was really hard to swallow. I'd already hired thirty new employees and rented a larger space. He knew better than anyone that I needed that cash to keep our expansion on track, but he demanded it back, anyway. It wasn't just my company he was giving up on, but me. Or at least, that's how it felt."

"That's horrible. I would have been incredibly angry with him, too."

"I was crushed! And now I find out it's because he chose Simone over me. He could have sold his books and paid for his treatment without having to pull money out of my company, but he chose to give them all to her, instead. That's what galls me the most."

Raven was growing increasingly agitated with every breath, her fists clenching and unclenching as she talked. There was something so angry and hurt about her words and posture. A sudden thought struck and exited my mouth before my brain could process it completely. "You knew about Simone being his daughter before the will was read, didn't you?"

She sighed and looked away.

Bingo! Raven had two motives—money and emotional trauma—to kill her dad.

"Talk to me, Raven, otherwise I'm going to have to tell the police about this, whenever they get here. Did you push that bookcase onto your father because of Simone?"

Raven began shaking her head so rapidly, I was worried she might actually give herself whiplash. "No, I didn't kill him. Even though I wanted to."

Her voice broke and she threw her head into her hands. "I flew over here to try to convince him to keep his money in my company, but he blew me off every time I tried to talk to him about it. Then suddenly, an hour before the party started, he pulled me aside to explain why he'd changed his mind. He said that I shouldn't take it personally, but that he'd canceled the auction sale, which is why he would no longer have any cash to invest. When I asked why, Dad said that he'd loaned them all to Wainwright so they could form the basis of some new literature museum being built on the East Coast. Before I could react, Dad blurted out that he had more good news—that Simone was his biological daughter. But he certainly did not mention that he'd already changed his will to favor her!"

Raven stopped and stared at the ground. "He was so excited about having a little girl. Can you believe it—he actually said that to me. I thought I was his little girl."

Before she could tear up again, I asked, "Not to be crass, but he did leave the house and his investment portfolio to the three of you. They've got to be worth several million dollars, right?"

"You would think. But Dad got this house for a steal because it had been on the market so long. Not many people want to shell out five million dollars for a villa in the middle of nowhere. It's going to take months, if not years, to sell the house, and I need the cash now."

I regarded the younger woman, her head now hanging low. It looked like she had the weight of the world on her slumped shoulders, but that didn't make her a killer, I realized.

"So what are you going to do—do you think you can still save your company, or are you going to file for bankruptcy?"

"If Tammy's right and there is nothing left in their accounts, then I'll have to convince a bank to invest in us, or start wooing more venture capitalists. At least green energy is trending right now, and I have a presentation ready for them to view. Otherwise I'm going to have to fire the thirty employees I just hired!"

Raven closed her eyes and breathed in deeply through her nose. When she opened her lids, I noticed how bloodshot her eyes were. "If you don't mind, I would like to have a few minutes alone."

"Sure, okay, take your time. We'll see you around."

As we walked towards the stairs, I looked to my partner, one eyebrow raised. "Do you think she killed her father?"

"No, I don't. She's in the same position as Roger—Harold being dead only complicates their need for cash, it doesn't alleviate it."

"You make a good point, Baroness. It looks like we can cross another suspect off of our list." As much as I wanted to keep Raven on it, there didn't seem to be any reason for her to kill her father.

Rich people problems, I thought. Try as I might, it was hard for me to feel sorry for her or Roger. My mom had felt lucky if she had enough to pay all of our monthly bills and buy groceries. But I did understand the pain of a loved one leaving you too soon, and all of those unanswered questions that would never be resolved. For me, it was why my father's family tried to gain custody of me after his death. For Raven, it would be why her dad stopped believing in her. I didn't know which was worse.

21

Wasted Search

We rushed up to the third floor, hoping to be the first to search Roger's room. The chances were slim, I realized, when we encountered several guests already upstairs, giggling as they ransacked each other's bedrooms and tore through their most private possessions. Apparently nothing was sacred in the search for millions of dollars' worth of manuscripts. My blood boiled at the thought of these well-dressed vultures pawing my clothes and undergarments, until I recalled that this was exactly why I always locked up my suitcase whenever I wasn't in the room.

"Why are they still searching for the books?" the Baroness said, asking aloud the question resting on the tip of my tongue.

"They must not yet have heard the news," I whispered back.

"Should we tell them?"

"No, let's let Tammy make that announcement." Despite my promise to the Baroness, I still hoped to find and secure the Avron Book of Hours before the police arrived. Getting it back now would be infinitely easier for Rosewood, I figured, than having to deal with Wainwright's legal team.

I only began to relax when we walked farther down the hallway and I noted that Roger's was the only door still closed. When I turned the handle, I discovered why. It was locked. I looked up and down the hall, but luckily those present were merely moving from room to room, and none seemed to be particularly interested in me or the Baroness. I pulled a bobby pin out of my hair, tucked behind my ear for emergencies such as this, and straightened it out. A few twists and clicks later, and we were in.

Once the Baroness was inside, I pulled the door shut and locked it again, hoping to have a few minutes alone to search before having to compete with the others.

"We better work fast; the rest are going to demand access as soon as they realize we're in here," my partner said.

"Good point. Why don't you search through the closet and the dresser drawers? I'll take care of the rest."

I took a second to study the room, taking in the silver platter on the writing table, its domed cover placed against the drawers. Next to it was a bottle of scotch and a single empty glass. However, there were no plates, bowls, or silverware present. I sniffed furiously, yet could not detect any lingering scents of food, either. If Roger had eaten something in here last night, he must have taken the dirty dishes downstairs already. But then why leave the silver platter and empty glass? Wouldn't it have been easier to use the tray to move everything downstairs at once?

The scene before me only reinforced my notion that Roger had used the platter to move the books upstairs, and not food. It was a clever idea. Thanks to his jet lag and late arrival, no one thought it strange that he was hungry so late at night—not even me, which was a bit worrisome. If I was going to make it through the rest of our assignments without mucking things up, it would do me good to be more suspicious.

We made quick work of the room, the Baroness whipping through his drawers as I checked behind every painting, under every rug, and behind every piece of vintage furniture I could move, in the hopes of finding a hidden space large enough to hold the five missing volumes.

Yet after ten minutes of intensive searching, we found nothing. I was considering how I could pry up a few floorboards when other guests began knocking on the locked door. Apparently, our exploration had not gone unnoticed.

"Let us in! We have as much right to be in there as you do, Lady Sophie!"

"The lock should keep them out. None of them are strong enough to break the door down without busting a shoulder or arm. Have you already checked under the bed?" the Baroness asked, one eye on the door.

"Of course I did. But Roger isn't dumb, or at least not enough to hide them in plain sight. And I also checked behind the headboard and between the box frame and mattress, for good measure, but found nothing."

The knocks at the door turned to pounding. Moments later, a particularly hard thump had the entire door vibrating. "Are they using a chair now?"

"It sure sounds like it. Well, I suppose we can let them in. It appears we were wrong that Roger took the manuscripts."

It was gracious of her to say "we," even though it was all me. "I was so sure he had brought them up to his room."

I sat back on my haunches and sighed, just as another scream filled the air.

22

Bingo!

On second thought, the cry that brought us both to our feet was more one of joy than terror. We rushed outside towards the source, a few doors down.

"I found them—all five of the missing books! Does that mean I get five discounts, or only one?" Belinda preened as she pointed towards under one of the beds.

Not wanting to be the one to dash her hopes, I ignored her question. "Whose room is this?" I asked.

"That funny little man with the handlebar mustache," her husband, Gary, replied.

My mouth dropped. "Do you mean Billy Sanders, the museum curator?"

"Yes, that's the one."

Belinda rushed out into the hallway and leaned over the railing, yelling out for all to hear: "We found the books. Billy Sanders took them. He's the murderer—grab him if you can!"

Her words caused a wave of giddy panic to ripple throughout the villa as her message was repeated down the staircase and floors.

"He didn't even try to hide them? They're worth millions, and he knows everyone is searching for them," I said aloud, but no one seemed to hear me. The other guests were too keyed up to listen, I think.

Moments later, Billy's voice resonated up the staircase as he ascended. "I heard my name. What are you yelling about?"

When he reached his open bedroom door and saw everyone inside, Billy's face turned fire-engine red and he began to sputter. It looked like he was going to self-combust or have a stroke at any second. "What is the meaning of this? How could you search through my things without asking my permission? Have you no decency?"

"That's the guy—grab him!" Belinda pointed, and two of the elderly guests grabbed the curator by the arms and pulled him further into the bedroom.

"Unhand me!" Billy struggled unsuccessfully, failing in his attempts to shake out of the older men's grip.

"We will, once the police have had a chance to interrogate you," Belinda said.

"What are you talking about? Why would the police want to question me?"

"Because the five illuminated manuscripts were under your bed this whole time, that's why."

His eyes bulged out of his sockets as he looked towards the bed. "That is ridiculous! Why would I steal what Harold had already promised to leave to my museum? I didn't know about the new will until after he had been murdered and the books had been stolen—just like the rest of you!"

"Look, sonny, all I know is that your director told Gary and me that if you did not come back to Boston with the Avron book, you were out of a job. And lo and behold, we found the missing books under your bed. It doesn't take a genius to figure out what happened."

"No!" Billy's voice sounded strangled.

"Would you hush up? Until we can turn you over to the police, we need to keep you constrained. So you better start cooperating, or else." The elderly woman tried to look menacing, but all she did was look constipated.

"Or else what?"

The woman's eyes widened as she looked around frantically, until she spotted a silver letter opener on the nightstand. She turned to face Billy, holding the letter opener as if it was a machete. "Or else I'll have to use this. Now get in the closet!"

Her husband opened the closet door, but closed it again. "I think the bathroom would be a better choice. We don't want him to try escaping during a toilet break."

"You can't detain me—this is kidnapping! I'm an American citizen—I know my rights!" Billy cried out.

Another collector held open the door to the bathroom. "In this case, it's a citizen arrest. Now get in there!"

When several elderly guests shuffled towards him, attempting to force Billy inside, he kicked at them and punched blindly. Unfortunately for the curator, he was in terrible shape and got winded quickly.

"I did not steal them! I'm being set up!" Billy leaned against the wall, panting. "A job isn't worth risking a prison sentence—I can always find another one! This is all a horrible mistake. I demand you call the police!"

"He's got a point. We better tell Tammy to let the cops know we have Harold's killer in custody," Belinda said.

"I haven't killed anything—not even a fly! Well, maybe a few flies and spiders."

"Tell it to the judge," crooned Gary as he squared his shoulders.

When Billy lashed out again, Jacques picked up a chair and held it up in the air, like a lion tamer would. Billy's howls, as his arms and legs made contact with the wooden chair, filled the room. Jacques slowly worked Billy into the bathroom's threshold, where another gave him a quick shove backwards and quickly shut the door.

Billy whimpered through the closed door, "I didn't do this. You have to believe me."

"Of course the killer would say that." Belinda pulled a high-backed chair close to the door and worked it under the handle.

She'd just finished, a satisfied smile on her face, when Tammy's voice made us turn to the doorway. "What in the devil is going on up here? Thanks to all that racket, I could barely hear the police."

"We found the books and the killer! Do I get a discount on all five, since I found them, or only one?" Belinda said.

"I didn't steal anything or kill anyone!" Billy's muffled cry was barely understandable through the door. "Let me out of here—you have no right to hold me against my will!"

COLLECTING CAN BE MURDER

Tammy pointed a manicured finger at the door. "Who is that?"

"Billy, the museum guy. He's the killer."

"No I'm not! Call the police—this is kidnapping!"

"I want no part of this," Tammy held up her hands and backed her way to the threshold. "The police are on their way, let's let them deal with Billy. As for the books, you'll have to talk to Wainwright."

After she turned on her heel and rushed out of the room, Belinda said determinedly, "Who the heck is Wainwright? We should go after her, Gary. She better not try to renege on her offer."

She turned to Jacques and another elderly guest. "Can you keep him constrained for a few minutes? We'll be back in a jiff."

"No! You can't keep me in here!" He pounded on the bathroom door as if his life depended on it.

"Are they allowed to restrain him, in such a way?" the Baroness asked me, aghast.

I shrugged. "It doesn't feel right, but I guess it is justifiable, until the police can get here to question him. The roads must be clear if the cops are on their way, so theoretically he could try to make a break for it."

"I suppose..."

"We better get him some cold cuts while we're down there. I don't want to be accused of mistreating a prisoner," Belinda stated, before looking to her cronies. "You will have to remain vigilant—we don't want any liberal-hearted guests helping him to escape." The way she squinted at me, I assumed that I was the liberal in question. Why did rich, old conservatives hate journalists so much, anyway?

I stayed put, regardless, hoping to be able to speak to Billy before the police arrived. But his captors were having none of it.

After a now-dejected Belinda and Gary returned with a selection of French meats and cheeses that would make any American prisoner jealous, I decided to forget about Billy and instead focus on the five missing books, now stacked neatly on top of Billy's bed. Could I remove the Avron prayer book without the other guests noticing? I shuffled towards the bed, trying to move slowly enough to be unnoticed, but no dice.

Gary sprung in front of me, as spryly as an octogenarian could. "Don't even think about it, missy. No one is going to steal them again, not on my watch. We may not be able to get a discount on any of them, but by golly, we are going to make certain that the police are able to return them to their rightful owner."

When he brandished his bristly hairbrush, I decided to leave the illuminated manuscripts be.

"Carmen, why don't we retire to the living room? I could use an aperitif," the Baroness said loudly enough for all to hear. Directly into my ear, she added softly, "Let's talk in our room."

I nodded and followed. Before we could reach the door, Belinda tapped me on the shoulder. "Wait a second, you are a journalist, aren't you? I bet this is the story of a lifetime, for someone like you. Seeing as I found the books, do you want to interview me later?"

"Umm…" On the one hand, I doubted Belinda or Gary could help me solve this mess, but experience had taught me that it was better to keep my options open. "Perhaps after the police arrive and we all gain a little more clarity."

Her smiled dissipated. "Sure, okay. You know where to find us."

23

Is He The One?

I left the scene, comforted by the knowledge that Billy wouldn't be able to get away from his elderly captors. They promised to stand guard until the police arrived, even if it took all night. I did not foresee much resistance from their captive. From the way Billy was snoring, his meal must have been to his satisfaction. Nevertheless, each had found an object to threaten the curator with, in case he woke up and managed to get the door open. Not that I expected him to test their mettle with their chosen weapons—a bristly hairbrush, walking stick, silver letter opener, and metal bookend in the shape of a puppy.

Streaks of sun lit up the hallway as we walked to our room. Through the windows, I could see several gardeners out, cutting up the fallen trees, their chain saws tearing through the thick branches with ease. Another was busy moving the bulkier bits off of the drive with a shoveler.

At this rate, I figured the driveway would be useable within the hour. Which was perfect timing. Once the police arrived and we could explain that the Avron Book of Hours had been stolen from the museum in Ohio, the Baroness and I would be able to head back to Paris for a bit of shopping and sightseeing before our next assignment. Sure, I would have loved to have turned it in to the American Embassy personally, but knowing it would soon find its way home was reward enough.

So why wasn't I clicking my heels in elation? True, the prayer book had resurfaced and appeared to be unscathed, meaning our mission was accomplished. Yet my need to see justice served had trouble seeing Billy pay for a crime he probably did not commit.

Once we were back in our bedroom and the door was firmly locked, the Baroness turned to me, a wide grin on her face. "It all worked out, after all! Once the police have taken the Avron prayer book into their custody, we can alert Rosewood. Reggie is going to be thrilled, and you should be, too!"

Lady Sophie's enthusiasm was infectious. A rush of pride filled my soul, making my spine straighten momentarily, until my concerns resurfaced. "Thank you. But do you really think Billy killed Harold to obtain the books? He did lie about why he flew over this weekend, which means he could have lied about his role in Harold's death. Yet, him being the killer doesn't feel right, despite his motive."

"You never know what someone is capable or, especially if they are pushed into an impossible situation. He could have killed Harold out of anger, or because he felt humiliated and betrayed by his change of heart," Lady Sophie insisted. "Or perhaps it was as simple as job security. It sounds like he's in trouble with his employer. But what does it matter? The police are on their way and are certain to take all five books with them, as evidence. So we are officially finished with this assignment, correct?"

I tried to shake the disappointment from my voice. "Correct."

"So why are we still discussing this?"

To avoid her gaze, I picked up a notebook I'd left lying out on my nightstand, now facedown on the floor. The other guests had done a thorough job of tearing apart our room, yet had not gone too crazy in their search for the books. Almost everything was slightly out of place, but nothing had been broken and the locks to our suitcases had not been forced. It was a good thing they were amateurs—anything locked was where I always began my searches.

I tossed the notebook back onto the nightstand, unable to let it go. "But would someone like Billy really kill to ensure his job's security? That's a very dedicated museum professional. Besides, if he really did steal the books last night, why not at least attempt to hide them, especially since he knew the rooms would be searched? Leaving them under the bed is an amateur move—unless someone is setting him up and wanted them to be easily found."

The Baroness paused as she seemed to consider my words. "I see your point. If Billy didn't take them, who do you think put them in his room?"

"My money is still on Roger. He could have moved them to Billy's room this morning while we were all downstairs eating breakfast. That would explain why we didn't find them in Roger's room just now."

"Ah yes, Roger. He is a gambler, which means he bluffs and cons people for a living. And there's that horrid watch and jewelry." The Baroness wrinkled her nose. I figured she would not like him, simply because of his profession, a vice she had seen destroy several of her friends' lives.

"Appearances do deceive, eh, Baroness?" I chuckled.

My emphasis on her meaningless title made her cringe. "How true. Carmen, you have to tell the police about your suspicions, otherwise Roger is going to get away with theft, and perhaps murder."

I nodded at her use of the singular pronoun instead of the plural. The Baroness was a useful ally to the Rosewood Agency, as long as no one suspected her of working for the organization. Not everyone in her circle of friends was enamored by its ongoing hunt for stolen goods, especially if it meant their own art collections could one day come under scrutiny. If word got out, she would be branded a traitor to her kind and expelled from her social network. "You are absolutely right. I will take care of it."

"So what do we do now?"

"Pack our bags, I guess, then wait for the police to arrive. With a little luck, we'll be on our way back to Paris before dinnertime."

I tossed my suitcase onto the bed and threw all of my possessions into it. The Baroness, however, was far more careful with her clothing, meaning it took her five times as long to pack the same amount of items.

Too keyed up to sit and watch her, I stretched out my back and yawned. "I'm going to rustle up a cup of joe. See you downstairs?"

"Sure thing. I'll just be a few more minutes…" the Baroness said as she glanced at the frocks still hanging in the closet. How all of that was going to fit back into her suitcase was thankfully not my problem.

24

French Casanovas

As I passed by the living room on my way to the dining room, I couldn't help but notice a group of guests chatting in a conspiratorial tone. I waved and walked past the door opening, before tiptoeing my way back to the threshold. Something about their tone and how they stopped talking midsentence when they spotted me told me I should listen in.

"I heard something positively delicious a few minutes ago," Countess Ursula said. "When I popped into the kitchen to ask for more orange juice, the help was gossiping about Simone in French. I didn't let on that I understood them, even though I do. So while they were pressing the juice, I hung around and sure enough, they kept talking."

I pushed my back further into the wall as I moved closer to the opening.

The woman's voice took on a mischievous tone as she continued. "Apparently no one is surprised to hear that Harold got a servant pregnant all those years ago. They said he was quite a good-looking young man and was known for being a bit of a Casanova. From the way they were talking, I wouldn't be surprised if he has children spread all over Europe!"

Ouch, I hope Simone didn't hear them gossiping, I thought. And here her mother thought Harold was the love of her life. Did Simone already know about her dad being a skirt chaser, and would it really matter to her now? All she wanted was a father figure in her life, and with her mother gone, it wasn't as if she had to worry about them butting heads.

"Speaking of Harold's kids…has anyone seen Raven? I tried talking to her earlier, but she was too angry to hear me out," George, the guy from New Jersey, said in his nasal voice.

"That one does have quite a chip on her shoulder," his wife, Ginger, added.

"That may be," George conceded. "But she is a brilliant computer scientist, and I'm having second thoughts about my decision to withdraw my investment. It's companies like hers that are helping to make green energy more feasible for the rest of us, through their innovative uses of technology."

Without fully thinking my actions through, I sprung into the room. Several guests gasped, and George paled considerably. "That's odd. Why would both you and Harold pull your money out of Raven's company, if it's got so much potential?"

"It's that reporter! Don't answer her, George!" his wife, Ginger, shrieked. "Were you eavesdropping on our conversation? You can't print anything you overheard in your magazine."

"Don't worry, I report on antiques, not the sordid details about the lives of those who collect them."

George tugged on his collar. "I should have talked to Harold before I took action. If I'd have known he needed the money for medical treatment, I would have left my money in her company. He had introduced me to Raven a few years ago, when she was searching for venture capital. I'd already agreed to help fund her again, along with her dad and a few other investors. But when Harold suddenly announced that he was pulling everything out, we all panicked and did the same."

"So Raven went from being fully funded to penniless, thanks to her dad's actions?"

"Yes, but you can't print that," George stuttered in, I hoped, shame. "I'll deny every word."

"My magazine would never print a story like this. You have nothing to fear."

"Alright." He seemed less nervous, yet still made a point of grabbing his wife's hand and pulling her out of the room.

My cover as a journalist was proving to be troublesome, now that our host was dead. Before I could catch anyone else's eye, the sound of gravel crunching under tires drew us all to the windows.

"The police have arrived!"

25

Nobel to the Rescue

The guests trampled down to the front door as soon as they spotted the police cars racing down the long drive, lights ablaze. The detective leading a pack of officers into the house was a dashing young man sporting a police jacket speckled with mud. He strode into the hall and seemed to pause to take in the scene before him, before announcing in a deep voice, "I am Detective Nobel. I wish to speak with Tammy Moreau."

Tammy leaned over the first-floor railing. "Oh, good, you're finally here. We have Harold's murderer locked up in the upstairs bathroom. Would you be so good as to follow me?"

Nobel ascended the stairs, a plethora of officers trailing behind him. Eager to see how this played out, I pushed my way towards the front of the group of guests and sprung onto the staircase, just behind the last officer.

Before we reached the third-floor landing, a hard pounding noise was audible.

"I'm being held against my will—help me!" Billy cried, his screams muffled by the door.

"Bull honkey—that man is a murderer, and we are the ones who caught him," Belinda said with pride as she nodded to her fellow octogenarian.

"I'm no murderer! This is all a misunderstanding—I'm the victim, not the perpetrator!" Billy maintained from inside the bathroom.

"Make room, everyone." The detective muscled through the crowd of elderly and pulled open the bathroom door.

Belinda got in a cheap shot with her purse and whacked Billy on the head as he exited. She wasn't strong, and the bag was not large, but it must still have been an unpleasant experience.

Billy alternately cried and raged at his captors, obviously traumatized by his brief captivity. "They should all be arrested for kidnapping!"

"It was a citizen arrest!" Belinda raised her bag menacingly, causing Billy to cower.

"I don't think this can really be considered kidnapping, more like involuntary entrapment," the senior officer mused. "Especially considering your captors believe you to be a murderer and thief."

"I did not steal Harold's books, nor did I kill him!"

"Then why were the missing books under your bed?" Gary asked, puffing his eighty-plus-year-old chest out as he did.

When Billy chest-bumped him, Gary went down like a bowling pin, taking Jacques with him as he fell.

"How dare you!" Belinda shrieked as she repeatedly slammed her bag onto Billy's back while the police tried to pull the men apart.

"My patience has reached its limit! Everyone downstairs to the living room!" Detective Nobel yelled over the ruckus, holding a pair of handcuffs high in the air, to emphasize his position and capabilities.

Once downstairs, the detective gathered all of the guests and household staff into the living room. After everyone was settled, he ordered us to be quiet while Tammy explained what had happened this weekend, starting with Harold's death and the theft of the five illuminated manuscripts. He jotted the information down in his notebook and reviewed it briefly before raising his head to meet our eyes.

After a long and uncomfortable staring contest, a quick round robin followed, during which he wrote down all of our names and connections to Harold. The detective's expression changed only slightly when Simone revealed that she was both a housekeeper and Harold's biological daughter.

"Alright, so everyone was invited to this private viewing because they had expressed interest in the illuminated manuscripts, except for Raven and

Roger. Is that correct?" He looked to Tammy for confirmation.

"Yes, and Billy." She looked at the curator, handcuffed and surrounded by police officers. "Come to think of it, Jacques was not here for the books, either—were you?"

"Er, no." The Frenchman in question was squirming in his chair. "I had expressed a desire to see his collection, but I could never afford to purchase any of his books. Harold had asked me to bring down some paperwork this week, and invited me to the party so I could see them before they were sold."

"What papers were so important that Harold asked you to hand deliver them instead of mailing them?"

The detective's question was innocent enough, yet Jacques broke out in a sweat and cast furtive glances at Tammy.

"He wanted to give a notarized copy of a sales contract to one of the guests, but the storm hindered the man's arrival."

"A sales contract for what exactly?"

"Harold's collection of twenty illuminated manuscripts to a collector named Roger Wainwright. But the sale was rather unusual in the sense that no money would change hands until after Harold died. Until then, the books would be on loan to the new museum Wainwright was building. I think their contract had to do with the insurance and upkeep, more than anything else."

"That is rather unusual." The detective regarded Jacques for longer than felt comfortable, before asking, "Why did Harold want to deal with all of these papers before the party? You would think he had enough on his mind, with his guests and the viewing."

"Harold wanted to get everything sorted out before he flew to the clinic next week to begin his treatment. He was not certain how long he would be in Switzerland, or if he would survive the treatments, and he wanted to know his books were safe and well-cared for."

Jacques's voice trailed off as Tammy stood up in a huff. "You knew he was ill, as well? Was I the only one Harold didn't tell? Unbelievable."

"Enough! Everyone needs to remain calm. Please return to your seat," the detective ordered, before looking to Jacques again. "Did any of the other guests know what you and Harold were doing in his office, or interrupt your meeting?"

Jacques seemed to hesitate before answering. "Harold was arguing with Billy when I arrived. It was all rather embarrassing, really. He claimed that Harold owed him something, and he refused to leave Villa Saint Marie until he had gotten what he came for."

"Why were you and Harold arguing, Billy?"

When the detective's gaze slid off of Jacques, I could see relief in the Frenchman's eyes.

"Harold had promised to bequeath the prayer books to my museum, but hadn't provided me with any written proof. He thought I should trust him at his word, but my boss wanted our agreement on paper. But Harold refused to provide me with one. I couldn't seem to convince him that my director demanded such a document and may have gotten a little agitated, but I didn't kill him!"

"Wait a second—" When Tammy began to speak, Billy shriveled into himself, as if he knew what she was going to say. "But Harold's new will states that all twenty had already been sold to Wainwright. Why are you lying to the police?"

Billy grew red in the face as Tammy spoke, yet remained silent.

"Who is to say that you didn't kill him last night, in the hopes that he had left the books to your museum in his will? This new testament is only a week old," Tammy added, making Billy turn inward even more.

"I just wanted to know why he changed his mind," Billy wailed and threw his face in his hands.

"You did kill Harold, didn't you?" Tammy gasped.

"No! But you are right about the donation. A few days before the party, he told me he changed his mind about bequeathing the books to my museum, but he refused to explain why. I flew over anyway to try to talk sense into him, but it was no use. He'd already sold them. I wasted my time coming out here."

"Why was this donation so important to you?" Nobel asked.

"Those blasted books are going to cost me my job—that's why!" Billy wrung his hands and looked up to the ceiling as he continued, as if he was too embarrassed to make eye contact with the detective. "My new boss wanted to buy the Avron prayer book as a publicity stunt, and he personally raised a million dollars in order to do so. Harold was not supposed to know about it coming up for sale, but we met up for drinks when he was in town for another auction, and I guess I had too many Mai Tais, because I opened my big mouth and the next thing I knew, Harold had swooped in and purchased the prayer book, right from under my boss's nose. When my boss found out what happened, he threatened to fire me! That's when I told him about Harold's intention to bequeath five prayer books to our museum. So he gave me an ultimatum—I could keep my job if I got it in writing."

When Billy paused to wipe his snotty nose onto his jacket's sleeve, Belinda saw her chance and whacked him over the head again. "I knew you were a bad seed!"

"Madame! If you cannot control your handbag, I will have my officer escort you back up to your room."

"No way I'm missing this," Belinda muttered and set her purse down on the floor next to her chair.

The detective turned back to his suspect. "Your boss threatening to fire you over the books seems like an extreme reaction."

"We don't exactly get along and I think he's using this as an excuse to get rid of me. But I love my job and don't want to be forced out!"

"Then Harold reneging on your agreement must have made you quite angry, Billy."

"I was furious! After all I had done to help him out over the years, this is how he rewards me? That's why I flew over to try to change his mind—with my boss's consent, mind you. You can call him and ask. He knows all about this fiasco."

"But you did threaten Harold—several guests heard you do so."

"Yes, I did—with words, not violence. Up until Harold made clear that my pleading wasn't going to work because he had already signed a sales contract with Wainwright. He even took me to his office and showed me the freshly notarized copy, after I said I didn't believe him."

"Did he say why he changed his mind?"

Billy shook his head. "No he did not, and I do not profess to understand the whims of the rich, which means I will probably never know for certain. When it was clear that nothing I could say would make him cancel the sale, all I wanted to do was leave. But the weather didn't permit that."

Tammy turned to Billy, a smug look on her face. "So you did kill my husband so you could steal those books. You just admitted you are out of a job without them."

"No, I didn't kill Harold or steal his books! Why will no one believe me?" Billy pleaded, throwing his arms up to the heavens.

"And yet the manuscripts that were found under your bed went missing at the same time Harold Moreau was murdered—yes?" Nobel asked.

"No!" Billy cried.

"Yes they were. I'm the one who found them so I should know," Belinda chimed in.

"And that is when you restrained him," the detective asked, for clarification.

"You bet we did." Belinda somehow saw the detective's statement as a green light to whap Billy over the head once more.

"Ow!"

"Enough! I am taking you to the station with us. Perhaps for your own safety, it is better." He narrowed his eyes at Belinda as she lowered her handbag, already poised to strike again.

"Officers, please take this gentleman out to the car."

"But I didn't do anything!" Billy dug his heels in when an officer tried to move him.

"Perhaps not, but the books were found in your room, and you and Harold were at odds over the ownership of five of the illuminated manuscripts. I assume you can understand why I wish to speak with you further. It would also be prudent for me to read through both the old and new last will and testaments, to learn more about Harold's intentions, before contacting your museum's director."

Billy threw his head into his hands again and began to weep.

The detective nodded once, and two officers dragged a screaming Billy outside. "Someone is setting me up! I didn't do this! Why will no one believe me!"

Billy's pleas were so convincing that I truly wondered whether the police really had their man.

26

Two Suspects Are Better Than One

We watched through the window as Billy resisted being put into the car, kicking and screaming as they dragged him towards it. After a struggle, the officers were able to peel his fingers off of the frame and close the door.

"Should I mention my suspicions about Roger to the detective?" I quietly asked my partner after the police drove off with a protesting Billy in the backseat.

The Baroness whispered, "This might not be the right time…"

I glanced over at the detective, who looked exhausted. I could imagine he had been up all night dealing with that harrowing storm and the aftermath. The last thing he probably wanted to have to do was investigate the death of a rich American collector. Before I could decide how best to approach him, Nobel turned to Tammy and asked in a weary voice, "I would like to see this new will, as well as the previous version. Do you have copies of both in this house?"

"Sure, I found them this morning in Harold's office. But none of us knew about the new will, until after Harold's death," Tammy insisted. "Follow me."

Countess Ursula pushed her way to the front of the group. "Now that you have the killer, can we finally leave this house?"

"Until we have had a chance to talk to Billy, contact his employer, and read through both wills, I am requesting—no, requiring—that everyone stay here. This case is too convoluted to release any of you, just yet. We will also be taking the five illuminated manuscripts with us, to dust for fingerprints and DNA evidence."

My heart skipped a beat when he mentioned the books. All I had to do now was contact Rosewood and our first assignment was as good as complete.

"Fine," Tammy said, "but as long as you're here, I want to file another complaint. Someone stole my turtle!"

"Excuse me, madame?"

"I can't find my turtle brooch. It's encrusted with diamonds and rubies and worth more than your annual salary, I suspect."

By the way the detective's expression darkened, her words had stung. Tammy, however, did not seem to notice that she'd insulted the man. "It's been stolen, and I want to file a report. My insurance company is going to want a copy of it."

"Madame, we are here to investigate your husband's murder. Can you let us focus on the task at hand before dealing with your missing trinket?"

Tammy's eyes narrowed. "Certainly, officer."

The guests began to shuffle away, grumbling as they went. However, the detective's next question caused them to pause and turn back around.

"Before you go, did anyone see Billy in the library around the time of the murder? Or see him taking the books up to his room the night of the party?"

No's all around. I could see the disappointment in the guests' eyes, wishing they had seen something useful so they could insert themselves into the investigation.

In the hope of helping the local police solve this more quickly, I piped up. "I doubt anyone could have moved the books out of the library on the night of the party. At least, not until late at night. They would have had to walk by a living room full of guests to reach the staircase. The killer must have hidden them somewhere in the library after the murder, and later moved them up to Billy's room, in order to frame him."

"Wait a moment—do you believe someone else committed the murder?"

"It is possible." I wanted to share my theory about Roger, but didn't want to accuse him of patricide without stronger evidence.

When the detective began to write my words down in his notebook, Roger coughed to get the officer's attention. "No one had to frame Billy. He could have killed Dad, hid the books in the library, and moved them up to his room after Mom and I went to bed. I did see a light on in his room last night, after I returned upstairs from my trip to the kitchen."

Something about Roger's arrogant tone made me snap. I was here in France trying to set several wrongs right, and this slimy eel was doing his best to get away with theft and perhaps murder. I couldn't let him slither away, unnoticed.

"Billy was stumbling drunk, so much so that you had to carry him upstairs. How could he have snuck back down to the library and retrieved the books, without anyone noticing?"

"But he wasn't passed out, was he? And I was down in the kitchen for quite a while preparing a royal meal for myself. Billy could have sobered up enough to have done it," Roger insisted.

The detective studied him longer this time. "Yet Billy was so inebriated that he couldn't climb the staircase on his own?"

"Yes, but Mom and I put him into bed fully dressed. And he was still singing when we left, so he was definitely conscious. He could have gotten up and went back downstairs," Roger maintained.

"Why did you fly over here this weekend?" I asked. "Earlier, in the library, you told me that your mother asked you to come because your dad was distraught about the upcoming sale. Just like you told the officer, here. Yet after the will was found, you acted like you were here to persuade your dad to bail you out of your financial problems again."

I knew it was not the place of a reporter to interrupt a police interrogation, but I wanted to get out of here. Yes, Billy had motive and opportunity, but he just wasn't the killing kind. Harold's son, on the other hand, was definitely hot-headed and cold-hearted enough to have offed his old man.

"Of course I didn't tell you the truth—my financial problems are a source of embarrassment, not pride. Why would I air my dirty laundry to a stranger?" Roger spat.

"When exactly did you arrive in the village?" Normally I wouldn't have pushed a suspect so hard—and especially not in front of a police officer—but

I was becoming convinced that he was our thief and killer.

"I don't have to answer your questions!" Roger snarled.

"The trains stopped running two hours before you knocked on the front door," I badgered, hoping to rile him up in front of the detective. "And you were the one who turned off the alarm when Jacques tried to leave in the middle of the night, so you know the current code. To top it off, I found one of your cufflinks under the fallen books. I bet it came off when you murdered your dad. So when did you really arrive at the house?"

Roger turned on me, his face a mask of rage. "How dare you accuse me of killing my own father! What's it to you, anyway? You're not the police."

"No, it is true she is not, but I am curious to hear the answers to this nosy woman's questions." The detective studied Roger as he spoke.

When the suspect remained silent, I kept pushing. "You claim that you went back downstairs to make yourself a meal, yet there were no dirty plates or food smells in your room. But there was a covered dinner tray, large enough to hold all five books. I believe that you used that platter to take the books upstairs last night, and then you moved them into Billy's room after we went down to breakfast. Jet lag was an easy excuse for you to sleep in later than the rest of us, so you had the upper floor to yourself, once we were all in the dining room."

I felt a little like Hercule Poirot, dazzling the crowd with my insider knowledge and deductions. The real fuzz, however, looked less than impressed. If anything, Nobel seemed downright suspicious.

Roger's cheeks flushed and his eyes narrowed to slits, but he kept his lips sealed.

Since he wasn't talking, the detective looked to me. "You are suggesting that Roger moved the books into Billy's room, *non?*"

"Yes." I nodded solemnly.

"This is ridiculous!" Roger sprung up in an explosion of anger. "I don't care what this woman says, I did not arrive at the villa until after my father's body had been found and his books were missing."

The detective stood up and nodded. "I believe there is one easy way to solve this mystery. We will dust the illuminated manuscripts for fingerprints.

You claim that you arrived after the books had been stolen, which means your prints should not be on them."

Nobel shouted something to his men, two of whom scurried upstairs with a toolbox-like kit. I only hoped they went light on the powder; I wasn't certain how the ancient covers would react to the chemicals. After they returned with several viable fingerprints scanned into a funky portable machine that resembled a smartphone on steroids, it was Roger's turn.

When the detective approached with the electronic fingerprint scanner, Roger looked up to Tammy. "Mother?"

She jerked her head at the police officer, as if to say, get on with it.

Roger's finger trembled so badly that another officer had to hold it still on the screen.

Seconds later, a happy ping emitted from the machine. After conferring with his officers, the detective locked eyes with Roger before announcing, "It seems we have a match."

"That can't be right!" Roger shrieked as two officers grabbed his arms.

"Yet, I trust this little machine more than you," Nobel said softly before bellowing, "Roger Moreau, I am arresting you on suspicion of five counts of theft and the murder of your father."

"I didn't kill anyone! Why would I? Dad's no good to me dead."

The detective looked to me. "Do you have a theory as to why Roger killed his father, Miss De Luca?"

"It's Mrs., and yes, I do. If he knew his dad was about to change his will to benefit another, it would be a strong motive to murder him before he could do so. Only, he was too late. Harold changed it a few days ago, but Roger didn't know that."

The detective's head swung over to Roger. Before he could say anything, his mother rushed over.

"How could you!" Tammy's slap rang through the room.

Roger pulled back, a sneer on his face. "Seriously? It was your idea to kill Dad this weekend and frame Billy for it. You're the one who removed the bolts from the bookcase—not me! And you gave me the new alarm code so I could sneak in and out without anyone seeing me."

Tammy shrunk back. "That's not true!"

"Stop it, Mother! You're only making things worse by lying," Roger said.

"Are you admitting that you killed your father, hid the books, and then rang the front door as if you had just arrived?" Detective Nobel repeated my summation, as if seeking confirmation from his prime suspect.

"No! It was supposed to happen like that, but I didn't kill him! Someone else saved me the trouble. The bookcase was already on top of him when I entered the library. So I decided to go ahead with the rest of the plan, anyway—which was to steal the five books Dad was going to give to Billy's museum. All I did is hide them behind other books in the library, not push over the bookcase. Billy still could have killed Dad, so his museum would inherit them. None of us knew about the new will."

"Or perhaps your mother pushed the bookcase over," the detective mused aloud, as he turned to Tammy.

Tammy held up her hands, as if trying to stop him. "Whoa, hold your horses. I admit to planning my husband's murder and to removing the bolts, but I did not kill him. That was Roger's job. I was dancing in the living room when the bookshelf fell."

In true sociopathic style, Tammy expressed no regret while admitting to such a heinous crime.

"Why did you want your husband to die?" Nobel asked in a quiet voice.

"Harold had grown distant and he was shutting me out emotionally, which made me suspect he was having an affair. We'd already had several nasty rows after he canceled the auction, and then I saw in his agenda that he had a meeting with his lawyer planned, to discuss his last will and testament. The idea that he would leave his possessions to anyone but me made me livid. So I decided Harold needed to die before he could change his will."

A single tear rolled down Tammy's cheek. "But I was too late. He left it all to a stranger. I have been married to him for thirty-two years. I deserved to inherit more than that liar."

"But Simone is not a liar, as you call her, but Harold's biological daughter," the detective pointed out.

"Oh, please. I bet she faked the DNA test somehow. Even if she is Harold's, my husband never mentioned getting any servant girls pregnant, so Simone's mother must not have meant anything to him."

I turned to Simone, standing at the back. She was now doubled over, her whole body shaking with sobs.

"Harold had talked about giving Billy's museum five of the illuminated manuscripts. I thought if Roger stole those, we could frame Billy for the murder, and Roger could sell the books in America, to pay off his debts. It was supposed to be a win-win situation."

"Not for Harold," I whispered to my partner. Unfortunately, she was not the only one who heard me.

"Speaking of which…" Roger turned to me, a wicked grin on his face. "Mom gave me a list of the five books Billy was supposed to receive. Four were in the display cases, but not the fifth. I panicked, thinking Mom had written the name down wrong, until I saw the Avron prayer book sticking out of your purse."

Roger whirled around to face the detective. "Why did Carmen, a supposed journalist, have one of Dad's million-dollar illuminated manuscripts in her bag? That's the question you should be asking, Detective."

I blushed, but kept my mouth shut, wishing I had done so earlier.

The detective, however, was not prepared to let it go. "We'll discuss Carmen's presence in the library soon enough. But considering her head wound, it is not probable that she pushed over the bookcase. You, sir, however, had opportunity and motive. I am taking you down to the station so I can record our conversation. Officers, please escort Mr. Moreau out to one of our patrol cars."

"But I didn't kill Dad! I admit, I intended to, but someone beat me to it."

"That may be so, but you do admit to stealing his books, which makes you part of this investigation. What I still do not understand is why you agreed to murder your father. Couldn't you have stolen the illuminated manuscripts and sold them off, without harming him?"

Roger's laugh was loud and bitter. "Are you kidding me? If Dad had survived, he would have listed them as stolen straight away, rendering them worthless. No reputable auction house would have wanted to touch them."

I widened my eyes, to keep them from rolling. the young man had a lot to learn about the art world.

Roger did not resist his arrest, as Billy had, but walked quietly out to the car.

When another officer placed a hand on Tammy's arm, the look on her face made him pull it back so fast, I was momentarily worried that she had bitten him. "You can't arrest me for planning a crime that did not occur."

Nobel paused, apparently considering her words. "Mrs. Moreau may remain at home—for now. But you are not to leave this house, for any reason. I am going to post my men at all of the exits to ensure that you do not."

27

Can We Leave Yet?

I applauded the police's thoroughness by taking both Billy and Roger in for further questioning, sensing this move would make it even easier for the Baroness and I to slip out of here.

"Since you now have two suspects in custody, surely we are all free to go?" Belinda asked.

The detective silently regarded the older lady, as well as the rest of the guests gathered around, waiting to hear his answer. After a few excruciating seconds, the detective responded in his quiet voice.

"Perhaps Billy killed Harold, or perhaps it was Roger. Or maybe neither of them did it, but one of you. I cannot rule out that we are dealing with two crimes—a theft and murder—that may have been perpetrated by two different persons. We need more time to untangle this mess, which is why I am asking you all to stay in this house for a little while longer."

"We have lives to get back to, you know. My business doesn't run itself," Jacques huffed as another guest nodded in agreement.

Detective Nobel raised his voice as his tone grew even more formal. "Ladies and gentlemen, I apologize if our murder investigation inconveniences you. However, you are all to remain at Villa Saint Marie until I have questioned both Billy and Roger. Their statements may lead me to call one of you in, for further clarification. I am assigning four of my men to stand guard at the exits to this house, to ensure you do stay. Please do not try my patience by attempting to leave. It will only make you appear guilty and I will be forced to take you in for questioning, as well. Before we leave, my officers and I will search through Billy and Roger's rooms. We wish to be left alone. Good day."

The detective nodded wearily to his gang of officers before leading them back upstairs.

When Belinda turned to the Baroness and said something snotty about the detective, I saw my chance to slip away and talk to Nobel about getting the Avron Book of Hours on its way back to Ohio.

The door to Billy's room was open and several officers were inside searching methodically through his things, photographing everything as they went. I admit, I was feeling pretty heady when I coughed in my fist to get the detective's attention.

I swear Nobel did a double-take when he noted who was standing in the doorway. "Ah, Mrs. De Luca. My deputy and I were just talking about you." The bemused expression on his face made me think that their conversation was not entirely positive.

"Oh, yeah? Were you saying nice things?" I began to step into the room, but he shuffled over fast enough to block my entrance.

He chuckled as he pulled a hand through his hair. "Who are you exactly? You mentioned that you are a writer for an antiques magazine, but most journalists I know try to remain neutral and on the sidelines, not accuse a stranger of murder in front of a detective, thereby inserting themselves into an active investigation. Who do you really work for?"

"Let's just say I appreciate seeing justice done, and I don't think Billy did it."

Nobel regarded me for quite some time before replying, "This case is quite messy, thanks to your involvement."

I blushed. "Thank you."

"That was not a compliment," he barked. "If you do not answer my question, I will be forced to take you to the station, as well."

My hope of playing my cards close to my chest disappeared instantly. "Look, I have not been entirely truthful with you. However, my true identity is on a need-to-know basis, okay?"

By the way the he rolled his eyes at me, I knew I had misjudged him.

"Can we cut out the James Bond act?"

This French detective wasn't going to be easy to bowl over. So I decided upon a more direct approach. "I'm an art and antiquities recovery specialist for the Rosewood Agency. It's a US-based organization that locates stolen objects around the world. I often go undercover as a journalist so that I can verify the object is the one we're searching for, before our lawyers get involved."

He leaned back on one heel to better study me. "You mean like Lara Croft?"

"She's more of a tomb raider, and not a real person," I said, taking into account the officer was easily twenty years my junior.

"How does one become an art recovery specialist? Did you work for the CIA or FBI? Or perhaps you still do?" By the smile playing at his lips, I got the impression Detective Nobel didn't really believe me.

I chuckled regardless. "No, nothing as interesting as that. I was bored with teaching art history at a local university when I met the owner of Rosewood Agency at an auction house I was considering working for. Before I could apply for the appraiser position, he had convinced me to work with his agency. Rosewood sent me here to find the Avron Book of Hours, one of the five books stolen from Harold's library that you now have in your custody. It was taken from a museum in Ohio ten years ago."

I did not mention that I had worked as an appraiser for several auction houses, as well as being on retainer at the Rosewood Agency. The freelance work had been the perfect way to fill my downtime while waiting for a new assignment and it also kept me abreast of any new developments in the world of art and antiques. Leads to finding stolen goods didn't come in every day, and I had preferred to do something more useful with my time than twiddle my thumbs while waiting for Reggie to call.

The detective cocked his head at me. "So you admit to coming here to steal one of our victim's illuminated manuscripts?"

My stomach clenched at his choice of words. "Not to steal, to verify the find. I'm only authorized to recover an object if I think it's going to disappear before our legal team can step in. In those rare cases, I take it to the proper authorities as soon as I can."

"So you say—we have at least one witness who says you had it in your purse when Harold was killed. I cannot recall seeing an alert about this stolen book possibly being in France."

"The cultural organizations we work for do not usually file a report with the police, because they do not want the theft to be leaked to the media. That kind of coverage tends to spark copycat crimes."

Instead of reassuring him, my answer only seemed to upset Detective Nobel even further. "If you were certain the book was here, why did you not inform the local authorities beforehand?"

"And risk Harold finding out why I was really coming to Villa Saint Marie? We received a tip that he bought an illuminated manuscript that may be the Avron Book of Hours we were searching for. There are seven in existence, and the books are practically identical save a few small details on the title page. For all I knew, he had bought a different Avron manuscript than the one we were searching for. We've learned the hard way how defensive owners can be. We have had instances of owners being so upset by the police's involvement that they destroyed the object in question, so that the investigation would have to be closed."

I gulped as I thought of my dear husband, knowing it was important to share his story, as well. "One situation even resulted in the murder of one of our agents, and since then my boss is even more careful to keep our involvement a secret."

The detective rocked on his heels as he studied me. "Okay, so let me get this straight—you claim to work for a clandestine organization that I've never heard of, one that does not have to answer to, or consult with, local authorities. And you recover"—he made invisible quotations around the last word before continuing—"antiques by means of theft, and justify your actions because the object was stolen from your client. Is that an honest summary?"

I tried for lighthearted. "When you say it like that, it does sound devious."
Big mistake.

"Americans! Even if you are telling the truth, your job does not give you a free pass to commit a crime—especially one on foreign soil! If this is the same book that was stolen from an American museum ten years ago, we will return it to its owner. I'm not handing a million-dollar manuscript over to a supposed agent of a secret organization."

"It's not a secret—"

"I've never heard of it, so it's secret to me," Nobel snapped. "If anything, your work as an operative for this clandestine organization moves you up my suspect list. Is murder justified, if it gets you the book back?"

"Of course not! To be clear, I am not asking you to hand the Avron Book of Hours over to me. I'm going to let my employer know where the book is, and ask him to contact you. He can explain why I am here and will certainly reassure you that I had nothing to do with these crimes."

"How can your boss be certain that you are not an agent gone rogue?"

My patience was wearing thin, and fast. "Look, Officer, I don't kill people. Heck, I don't even carry a weapon. And I certainly do not steal things."

"It's 'detective,' and you don't need a weapon to kill someone. I've seen those spy films. If you are trained properly—by, say, a secret organization..." He raised an eyebrow and sneered, clearly badgering me. "You could have pulled the bookcase onto both of you, in order to divert suspicion from yourself."

As much as I wanted to smack that sneer off his face, I had to do whatever it took to make him lose interest in me, even if that meant being humble—not my strongest suit.

I sighed and held up my hands in defeat. "I can tell we aren't going to get anywhere..."

"No, we are not."

"Then I guess you'll have to trust me at my word—that I am not a thief or killer, and I promise not to leave France anytime soon." I gave him my most winning smile. It took all of my willpower not to raise two fingers above my eyebrow in a Girl Scout salute.

"Or I can confiscate your passport and send your photograph and details about your work and employer to all ports of entry and exit in Europe."

My jaw dropped automatically.

He held out his hand. "Your passport, *s'il vous plaît.*"

"You're wasting your time investigating me," I grumbled as I rooted around in my purse.

"I will admit, you are not a prime suspect, yet. However, your interest in the Avron book and your being at the scene of the crime make you a person of interest. I expect you to stay in this house for the time being."

I held my tongue and let my head droop; that was as humble as Detective Nobel was getting. After digging through in my purse for longer than plausible, I finally pulled out my passport and handed it over.

He squinted at the details printed in my passport, as if he was trying to discern from my photograph whether I was telling the truth or not. "Give me time to call your Rosewood Agency, and I will get back to you later."

"Understood. I'll alert my boss and I bet he'll get in touch with you within an hour or so."

The detective grimaced. "I can't wait. Now, if you will excuse me, I have a murder to solve."

28

Calling It In

I retreated into the hallway and stared out the windows after the detective's dressing-down, trying to process what had just happened. Minutes later, Nobel, with the stolen books in hand, led his gang of officers down the winding steps and out to the awaiting patrol cars.

As they sped away, I tried to stay positive. The police now had the Avron book, which meant it would be returned to its rightful owner, as soon as all the legal mumbo jumbo had been dealt with.

It was a clear win for our team. So why didn't I feel proud or elated?

Being a suspect in Harold's murder didn't help, but a chat with my boss would clarify my role in this fiasco. Perhaps my sullen mood was because this was the first time I could recall messing up an assignment so badly.

Before my husband's murder caused my world to collapse, I had been one of Rosewood's most effective agents. I used to be able to fly under the radar, verify the object, and alert Rosewood, all without the local PD noticing my presence. Yet, during my first job back after three years of being out of the game, I had stumbled right into a murder investigation. It was simply bad luck, I supposed, but still frustrating.

My only hope was that either I or the police figured out who killed Harold, before Nobel had a chance to spread my information around Europe. If he did, I might as well pack up and go home. It would ruin my chances of remaining incognito and render me useless to my employer.

When I opened the door to my bedroom, the Baroness was propped up in bed, reading a magazine.

"Whatever is the matter?"

"Is it that obvious?" After I told her about my exchange with Detective Nobel, my normally unflappable partner exploded in anger.

"Why did you expose yourself to him? All you had to do was call Rosewood and let them handle it!"

I sat on the edge of the bed, puzzled by her intense reaction. "I guess I was a little gung ho, but I figured we could save our lawyers and the French police some time by explaining why I had the Avron book in my bag, so they wouldn't feel compelled to investigate me."

"That worked out swimmingly, didn't it?"

"Cut the sarcasm, Baroness. I didn't mean to upset you or our employer. What happened during my absence that's got you so upset?"

The Baroness waved my question away. "It doesn't matter now. We have to call this in so somebody at Rosewood can contact Detective Nobel."

I shook my head and stared at the ground, knowing I was being juvenile. "I don't want to. Can't we wait and see what the police get out of Roger and Billy first?"

The next time I called my contact at Rosewood, I wanted to have good news to share—not this screw up. Right now, I didn't know which filled me with more dread—being a murder suspect or having to tell Myrtle about it.

"There's no time to dally. Myrtle needs to get the lawyers on the phone to the detective as soon as possible. That's going to be our best hope of getting out of here, with your cover still intact."

The Baroness dug through my purse until she found my phone, then dialed Myrtle before handing it to me. I snatched the ringing phone out of her hand, then stepped away so I could have a little more privacy. Myrtle and I had a complex relationship, but were both consummate professionals who would never endanger our mission simply because we disliked each other. At least, I hoped we both were.

"Dislike" may be the wrong word. I guess I didn't like phoning Myrtle because I always felt like I was talking to a disappointed mother figure. I dialed and waited for her to answer, wondering when the first insult would drop.

"Ah, knucklehead. I can't believe you're out in the field again. Poor Reggie must be really short-staffed to have asked you back."

Her insulting gibes only conjured up a sense of nostalgia in me.

"Myrtle, trust me, there was no one else available."

"Okay, spill it. Are you still in Villa Saint Marie?"

Five minutes later, after I finished my story, I realized with glee that I had accomplished the impossible—Myrtle was speechless. Several glorious seconds passed before she finally responded. "You had the Avron book in your bag, and the cop knows it? Ah, Carmen."

I heard her drop the phone and a few choice words, followed by the clinking sound of coins against glass. Myrtle's foul tongue had been slightly tempered by the "swear jar" her son, my boss, had placed on her desk. The proceeds went to the coffee fund, and thanks to Myrtle, the head office owned one of the fanciest espresso machines I'd ever laid eyes on. The delicious smell of freshly ground beans was always a welcome treat whenever I stopped by headquarters.

"I didn't have a choice. Harold swore he'd only split up the collection over his dead body. He didn't mention having sold it to another collector," I yelled into the phone, hoping she could still hear me.

A rustling noise made clear she was picking the receiver back up.

"You always have a choice, and recovery is a last resort." Her deep disappointment carried through the phone line.

I shook my head, confused by how resolute she was being. "I don't understand—Reggie always trusted my choices before. It's not like I expected to be knocked unconscious before I could hide the book in my luggage." I heard the whininess in my voice but couldn't help it. My professional pride was bruised beyond belief.

"We've had a few incidents since you've been out of the picture, and discretion has become more important than retrieval."

"What are you talking about?"

"Our reputation with European law enforcement agencies is a little tarnished, due to a recent incident. I'm surprised Lady Sophie didn't mention it to you, or remind you to stay out of the investigation. We don't want this detective showing an interest in you and possibly blowing your cover and, as a result, the next mission."

I was glad we were talking via the phone line, not in a video call. If Myrtle saw how red my face was right now, she'd never let me live it down. The Baroness had repeatedly warned me to exercise caution, yet I hadn't really listened because she refused to fully explain why.

"It's not Lady Sophie's fault. I'd taken the initiative and talked to the detective about the book, without consulting with her first. Besides, it might be too late. The next mission may already be compromised. The detective took my passport because he considers me a suspect," I added under my breath.

"He what?" Myrtle's shriek rang through the line. "Then you have to un-suspect yourself—prove you are not the murderer by figuring out who did kill the guy. Then play nice with the detective so he gives you back your passport and forgets about you. I'm not even going to tell our boss about this mess, but I am sending a team of lawyers over to retrieve the book."

"I don't want to play detective!"

"And your employer doesn't want you to be a suspect in a murder investigation. If the police investigate you, Rosewood will come under scrutiny, as well. It's not entirely legal what we do, is it? So you have little choice but to get sleuthing."

"I'm really sorry, Myrtle. I thought taking the Avron manuscript would help wrap up our end of the case sooner, not get us further involved in it."

"It looks like you were wrong about that."

Before I could retort, the phone line went dead. As soon as Myrtle hung up on me, I turned to my partner.

"Myrtle told me there have been a few recent incidents that make retrieval less of a priority. What does she mean and why didn't you warn me about them earlier?"

The Baroness raised an eyebrow at me. "Don't try to put the blame on me. There were a few incidents, none of which I thought would have any bearing on our assignments. But then, I didn't expect you to do something as silly as tell the police who you really are."

I counted from ten to one backwards, to cool off, before asking, "What happened while I was gone?"

The Baroness sighed softly and looked away before answering. "There were a few, but the worst was a situation with an overeager rookie agent working in Italy. To make a long story short—an agent verified a statue and saw it was about to be auctioned, so he took it. It turned out, the Italian art police had the seller under surveillance and our agent inadvertently mucked up their operation. The bad guys were tipped off and went underground, with the rest of the stolen statues. The authorities were so angered by our actions, they told the media all about the Rosewood Agency, but in the most negative terms. The press had a field day with us, and the articles made us look like a bunch of bumbling amateurs. The trust we had built up with several law enforcement agencies has been under strain ever since. Which is why Reggie would prefer we operate under the radar whenever possible."

I considered her words and my actions over the course of the past few days. If I had known about this mishap, I never would have put that Avron prayer book in my bag. "This is going to make my job even more challenging."

"True, that's why they pay you the big bucks."

I stared hard at my partner, knowing she was teasing, even though it felt too soon for her to do so. "I need a coffee. Should we get a cup before we discuss the suspects?"

29

Avoiding Jail Time

The Baroness popped into the bathroom to freshen up, giving me a few welcome minutes to sort out my head. Being a person of interest was not the development I sought in my first job back. Part of me wanted to be angry with her for not telling me about the incident earlier. However, I knew all too well that there had been little time for her to do so.

After the Baroness convinced me to help her out with this whirlwind tour of Europe, I had spent a week preparing for our first assignment—the Avron Book of Hours—and most of that time I had spent online, buttering Harold up so he would agree to an interview. I had little contact with the Baroness until I arrived in Paris, a few hours before we drove down to the Brittany coast together.

We had taken turns sleeping and driving, knowing we were expected to be jovial and chipper as soon as we arrived at Villa Saint Marie, not jet-lagged. During the few minutes we had both been awake, we gossiped about former co-workers and rehashed old cases, instead of discussing anything more recent or personal.

Since arriving here, our time alone had been spent feeling each other out as we tried to get back to where we had been, before my husband died and the Baroness turned her back on me—just two professionals united by a love of art.

It was no wonder she failed to mention the change in company policy or the reasons for it. I knew I needed to forgive Sophie so we could do what Myrtle asked—figure out who killed Harold and make nice with the detective in the process. Our next assignment was in Belgium in a week's time. I didn't want to be in a jail cell, instead.

30

Motives Galore

After we had fueled up on caffeine, I felt confident we could puzzle out the murderer before Detective Nobel did. Unlike him, we had been here the entire weekend, locked in this house with all of the suspects.

We headed back up to our room, so we could talk more freely. As soon as the door closed, the Baroness asked, "If Billy or Roger did not kill Harold, who did?"

She looked to me as if I already knew the answer.

I twisted a strand of my long hair around my finger, considering who else could have done it. "The only other ones who stand to gain, or thought they did, are Raven, Simone, and Tammy. Since we've already questioned Raven and neither one of us thinks she had a strong enough motive to off her dad, that leaves Tammy and Simone."

"Let's start with Tammy. Her confession to the police could have been a double-bluff. After all, she did admit to planning on killing her husband, and is strong enough that she could have pushed the bookcase onto you and Harold."

I nodded slowly. "True. If she was concerned that Roger wouldn't be able to reach the house, because of the storm, she may have decided she had no choice but to do it herself. It does sound like she wanted Harold to die last night, while all of the guests were still here, so there would be more suspects."

"She did make a point of telling everyone she would be searching for paperwork in Harold's office, instead of the books," the Baroness pushed. "If one of us found them, she could claim that it proves she didn't know where the books were, which would support the idea that she could not have stolen them," she continued.

"That's devious, I like it." I chuckled as I regarded my partner. From the tilt of her chin, I had the impression that the Baroness was convinced that Tammy was our culprit. As much as I wanted to agree, we had another suspect to consider. "That leaves Simone."

Just saying the words aloud made my stomach clench. Of all of the possible suspects locked up in this house, Simone had the most to gain. Yet there were so many similarities between our life stories, I could not help but feel protective of her. "Why would she murder Harold? She'd desperately wanted to get to know her biological father, and she finally had her chance to do so."

"So she says. However, Harold was about to fly to Switzerland, and it was not certain if he would ever return," reasoned the Baroness. "Simone could have felt as if he was abandoning her again and lashed out. But let's not forget, the sale of the book collection was contingent on Harold's death. She has thirty million reasons to kill him."

I nodded, trying to be objective, but my heart refused to accept that Simone could have done it. "She did say Harold promised to change his will to benefit her, soon after they received the results of the DNA test. But did she know that Harold had already gotten all of the paperwork in place? If she did, then she is probably our killer. If she did not, then she would not have a motive."

"You're right. She did seem quite surprised that Harold had already changed his will to include her, so I suppose she did not know about the new version." The Baroness almost sounded disappointed.

"There you go, she can't be our prime suspect," I said quickly and with relief. "I say we focus on Tammy for now."

The Baroness studied my face, a frown on hers. "Wait a moment—you aren't going to confront her, are you? If she really did kill her husband, that may be dangerous. I would go with you, but..."

My thoughts flew to my husband, wondering what tragic set of choices had led to his death. If he had refused to go to that meeting alone, would he still be alive today? Or would his killer have taken his life, and that of his partner, instead?

"No, that's a bad idea. If Tammy did not kill her husband, we can't risk her finding out that you're working for the Rosewood Agency. She's too well-connected. It would only take one word to the right gossipmonger, and all of Europe's cultural elite would know that you are helping me to infiltrate their parties—and why."

"Then what do you suggest we do?" my partner asked.

"I think a gentle approach is our best bet. Let's probe the other guests first, to see if we can find out more about their movements the night of Harold's death. Perhaps someone saw or heard something out of the ordinary that would help the police pin this on Tammy. With a little luck, one of them will provide the clue we need to solve this thing."

"Why would they open up to us, and not the police?" the Baroness asked.

"Because we aren't the cops and we can't arrest them. I think you'll have to take center stage for this next bit. My cover as a journalist is making some of the guests nervous. I'll stay in the background and listen in for now. If this doesn't work, I'll figure out a safe way to confront Tammy."

The Baroness touched her tiara, then raised her chin. "Alright, I'll ask what the others think about Billy's and Roger's arrests, and then shift the conversation back to the night of the party. How does that sound?"

"Like an excellent plan," I lied. It didn't sound like much of a plan, at all, but it was the best I could come up with at the moment. And doing something was far better than doing nothing.

31

Plugged Ears

Before we could exit our bedroom, my phone began ringing. When I saw who was calling, a smile lit up my face. "I should take this. I'll be downstairs in a minute."

The Baroness waved before pulling the door closed. As soon as I answered, Rhonda's voice filled my ears, her irritation audible through the phone line.

"Where are you? I'm standing courtside and our drinks have been served. Your ice is melting."

In my haste to prepare for this last-minute assignment, I had completely forgotten to call my bestie and tell her I couldn't make our weekly tennis date. Serena and Venus Williams had nothing to fear when we stepped on the court, but Rhonda and I enjoyed batting the balls around as we gossiped about our friends and loved ones.

"Shoot. I'm really sorry, Rhonda, but I can't make it. I'm in France."

"My ears must be plugged up because I swear you just said you were in France."

"Can I make it up to you with a mini-Eiffel Tower?"

"Do you mean one of those little statues made of metal?"

"Indeed. You get to choose the color."

"Pewter, please. Are you going to tell me why you are in Europe—and without me?"

"Great, pewter it is. I'll see if I can find one with fake diamonds embedded in the tower. They do sparkle so," I replied, ignoring her question. "By the way, have you checked your email lately?"

Rhonda was quiet a moment, before she said in a soft voice, "Now that you've retired, I thought you were done with all that lying and sneaking around. You are still retired, aren't you?"

As much as I wanted to confide in my best friend, I knew my company's confidentiality agreement didn't allow it. When I remained steadfastly silent, she sighed and mumbled, "It doesn't matter. No, hon, I haven't checked my email at all this week, not since my show went on hiatus. All I've been doing is lounging around my pool, trying to recoup from this hectic season. Today's the first day that I've pulled on anything but a bikini!" she guffawed.

On Rhonda's hit television show, people brought in their antiques and collectibles to have my best friend appraise them live, on air. Most hoped that their trash was treasure, but those cases were few and far between. The program's popularity had as much to do with her bubbly on-screen personality as it did her keen eye and expansive knowledge of art and antiques.

"I'm sorry I'm not there to beat you at tennis again."

"Are you getting old on me? Your memory must be getting faulty if you think you won the last time we played."

"Fair enough. We'll battle it out, as soon as I get home."

"Before you go—what did you email me? I promise to check my computer later, but can you give me the short version?"

"Your show is a hit here in France! The staff at the house we are staying at is crazy about you."

"Golly, that's really sweet. I'll have to send over some signed photographs. How long are you going to be there, or is that a secret, too?"

That's the question of the hour, I thought. "Not much longer. We're off to Belgium next week, but maybe you can send the staff a card, anyway. I'm sure they'd love it. I'll send you the address."

"France and Belgium? I'm so jealous! I sure wish I could go on an adventure like you. Let me know if you need an assistant or anything, alright?" Rhonda's belly laugh filled the line.

I chuckled along, knowing that my boss would never allow a civilian to help out on a mission. "Sure thing. Listen, I better get back to work. We'll catch up on our tennis matches when I'm back in the States."

"I'll hold you to it. You take care now."

32

Showdown at Villa Saint Marie

I sprinted downstairs to find the Baroness already in the living room, working the guests like a pro, so I popped into the dining room to see what I could overhear. Before I could approach anyone, angry voices coming from the second-floor landing drew me out into the hallway. It sounded like two females, and my money was on Tammy and Simone. By the time I reached the first-floor landing, several guests were gathered around, open-mouthed as they watched the two women duke it out verbally.

"You are still my maid!"

"Housekeeper! And I quit already. You're going to have to clean up after yourself for a change."

"Then get out of my house!"

"Not until the books are safely delivered to their new owner."

Tammy suddenly turned and screamed up the staircase, "Jeeves! You know what to do."

"What's that supposed to mean?" I mumbled, seconds before the butler appeared on the stairs, luggage in his hand.

When he reached the first floor, Simone snarled, "Is that my suitcase? Did you touch my things?"

She pulled the bag out of his hands and threw it on the floor. "You had no right to touch my possessions." She dug through her neatly folded clothes until she found a small, zippered bag.

"I bet you stole Tammy's brooch," Simone snapped. "You're always sneaking around, poking through other people's things."

The butler's eyes bulged out of his sockets, showing the most emotion he had since I'd arrived. "I'll have you know that I have never —"

"It's alright, Jeeves," Tammy called out. "I trust you implicitly. I know you would never take my turtle. This one, however…"

Simone ignored Tammy and tore the bag open. She seemed on the verge of tears, until her fingers encircled a gold chain. "Thank goodness, my mother's necklace is still here."

"You're luckier than me. I still can't find my brooch," Tammy grumbled. "Now take your things and leave my home."

The other guests watched in mock-horror, but I could tell they were reveling in being front and center for this juicy fight.

"No, Tammy," Simone snarled, emphasizing her employer's name. "I don't work for you anymore so you can't boss me around. I am not leaving here until the books have been picked up. Until then, I am their caretaker, and that means I need to be where they are. Which means I'm staying, for now."

"Over my dead body," Tammy yelled.

"That can be arranged—I'll soon be rich enough to make that happen," Simone hissed.

Tammy paled as she stumbled away. When Simone burst into tears and rushed off, presumably to the library to be with her books, the other guests and I retreated to the living room.

Conspiracy theories and much speculation flew around the room. Once everyone had gotten the latest scandal out of their system, the conversation turned back to the police and weather. Unfortunately no one provided any new nuggets of information that would help prove that Tammy had murdered her husband.

I slipped upstairs, hoping to catch up with Jeeves. Luckily for me, he was dusting the second-floor hallway. However, he was as tight-lipped as they came, and steadfastly refused to discuss Simone, Harold, or his employer's family to strangers, despite my most charming interrogation techniques.

Since he refused to divulge any family secrets, I had to resort to plan B. It was time to confront my suspects. Tammy was a heartless wench who had expressed almost no emotion concerning her husband's death, and had even admitted to planning to do him in that same night. She could have easily have pushed the bookcase over, before Roger arrived.

To me, she had to be our killer, simply because I could not accept that Simone had done it. My heart told me that she could never hurt the father she had just been reunited with. Yet my head reminded me that anyone was capable of murder, with the right incentive.

As it stood, I couldn't rule either woman out.

33

Eeny Meeny Miny Moe

Since one or both of my remaining suspects were not telling the truth, I had to figure out another way to solve this crime. There was always the chance that Billy or Roger had done it, but I'd have to wait for the police to sort out their motives and movements. Until then, all I could do was try to determine whether either woman was our killer.

As I started downstairs, the bitter scent of cigarette smoke reminded me of one more loose end to follow up on. I changed direction, figuring the source of the stinky smell was Jacques using the rooftop terrace as his smoking lounge. Money was at the heart of this matter, it seemed, and I had a few unanswered questions about Harold's paperwork that he might be able to clarify.

Sure enough, Jacques was up there, enjoying the sun and a smoke. He waved when I approached, but his smile froze after I spoke.

"Why did you lie to the police?"

Jacques began to puff up his chest, as if to deny it. However, my patience was worn too thin to play games with him.

"Please don't waste any more of my time. You told the police that you had dropped off a notarized copy of a contract for Harold, but it was more than that. You were here to witness him signing his new will, weren't you?"

Jacques began to shake his head, as if to deny it, but suddenly stopped and threw his hands up in the air, instead. "What does it matter now? Fine—you

169

figured me out."

"Why didn't you tell the police the truth?"

"Harold did not want his wife to know about the sale of his collection, or the existence of a new testament, until both documents had been notarized. You have met her—I did not wish to tell the police this in front of her, because I am scared of that one. You saw how she reacted when she discovered I already knew Harold was going to Switzerland for medical treatment."

I chuckled. "She does make her feelings known. Back to the will, don't you need two people to witness Harold's signature? Or does your capacity as a notary make that superfluous?"

"No, two witnesses are required. In this case, Harold asked two of his kitchen staff to witness his signature."

"Alright, thank you." Could the two staff members have told Tammy about the new will? Our hostess did not strike me as someone who inspired loyalty in her employees.

If the two witnesses had told anyone, I realized with a sinking heart, it would have been the main beneficiary—Simone. The three did work together on a daily basis and appeared to get along, at least in front of the guests. Although if I was in their shoes, I would be awfully jealous that Simone was about to inherit so much money. Perhaps they did not say anything, simply out of spite.

"You will say nothing to Tammy about this?" Jacques begged.

Part of me wanted to toy with him and say that I would, but his pleading puppy dog eyes convinced me otherwise. "I promise not to say anything to her—as long as you tell the police the real reason you came to the villa this weekend. It might help them solve the murder."

34

Expat Dreams

After getting Jacques to promise he would contact Detective Nobel straight away, I trotted down the stairs to the kitchen. I didn't know what the two staff members could tell me, but it felt important to find out. For all I knew, they could provide the clue that broke this thing wide open.

If they did not, I wasn't certain how this European adventure was going to end. So far, I had not found a smoking gun pointing me to the killer. And if I was coming up empty-handed, I bet the police were having even less luck. Which meant we would be here for several more hours, if not days. How long would it be before the detective decided to spread my face and employment history around Europe?

As frustrated as I felt, the possibility that someone like Nobel could clip my wings only made me more determined to get this situation resolved.

Before I reached the kitchen door, Tammy exited, a mimosa in hand. The way she wobbled on her heels as she made her way to Harold's office made me think that this was not her first drink of the day.

Despite my promise to the Baroness, I couldn't pass up this chance to confront Tammy. She was ruthless enough to have planned her own husband's murder—who's to say she didn't actually commit it?

So I followed slowly behind and waited until she'd entered Harold's office before making my presence known. I knocked on the open door before poking my head inside. "Hi, Tammy. How are you doing?"

Tammy was sitting behind Harold's desk, her drink in one hand and a picture frame in the other. She looked up from the photograph, her eyes watery from booze and emotions, I figured. "What do you want?"

"To see if you are alright. I can imagine things didn't quite go as you expected this weekend."

Tammy snorted. "That's the understatement of the year. Are you really a reporter? You and Detective Nobel seem to be getting along quite well."

"I really do work for *Hidden Treasures*; you can look up my bylines online," I said with confidence, glad my cover included articles credited to me in the magazine. "But we don't print gossip or report on murders, only stories about interesting and valuable collections. Right now, I'm reaching out to you as a woman who has also recently lost her husband. Nothing more."

Tammy's mask of arrogance seemed to dissipate momentarily. "When did he pass?"

"Three years ago, but it feels like yesterday," I whispered as a wave of sadness washed over me.

"That's tough, especially if you still loved him. I suppose you did, didn't you?"

She looked to me for an answer, but all I could do was nod, unable to say anything for fear of my voice breaking.

Tammy lifted up the frame in her hand, turning it so I could see the image inside—a snap of her and Harold on their wedding day. "This was the best day of my life. I had no idea it was going to go downhill from there."

She stared at the image as she spoke, almost as if she was trying to communicate with Harold, instead of me. "That servant is three for three. I didn't know about her, or that he was diagnosed with cancer and was flying to Switzerland for treatment. He even kept his deal with Wainwright from me, but she knew all about it. Apparently our thirty-two years of marriage meant nothing to him."

When she tossed the framed photograph onto the desk, a stack of paperwork in an open folder shifted but didn't fall to the floor. I twisted my head to better read the top document.

"Are those the titles to Harold's illuminated manuscripts?"

"Yep. I found them in a folder entitled 'Wainwright,' along with a notarized copy of their agreement. Harold had already arranged for them to be transported to Wainwright's new museum in the States. I guess he wasn't going to mention it to me until the delivery driver showed up. Part of their agreement is that the books be displayed in a hall bearing Harold's name! Can you believe it? It wasn't just the money, but the idea that his name would live on, that must have made him seal that deal with Wainwright. It also explains why he pulled the books out of the auction and reneged on his promise to Billy's museum."

Tammy looked to the desk and sighed. "And here I thought he was leaving me for another. This is so much worse."

"I'm so sorry." As much as I disliked her, I could still sympathize with her pain. Finding out your partner in life had repeatedly lied to you must have been heartbreaking.

She took another swig of her drink, momentarily drowning her sorrows. "Maybe Simone was telling the truth about being his biological daughter. It's a good thing she didn't meet him earlier—he was a horrible father; just ask Roger or Raven. Harold was always more interested in finding the next big thing than spending time with them."

I studied Tammy, now several shades from sober. Yet, try as I might, I couldn't bring myself to feel sorry for her or Harold's kids.

"What are you going to do now?"

"According to their agreement, the proceeds from the books' sale will be deposited in a trust fund he set up for Simone. My lawyer thinks he may be able to prove that Harold was mentally unstable when he changed his will, given the advanced state of his prostate cancer and the sudden appearance of his daughter. He's going to argue that the emotional shock caused him to make an out-of-the-ordinary decision that is not in keeping with his true intentions. But I'm not holding my breath."

"So he was terminally ill?" I asked.

"Apparently he was on death's doorstep. That explains his sudden weight loss and mood swings." Tammy reached over the desk and rummaged through the pile of papers, until she found a folder and tossed it over to

173

me.

"I've found all of the medical appointments in a folder marked 'Geneva.' He had a one-way train trip booked to Switzerland next week. And according to this medical referral, he was going to take part in an experimental treatment for prostate cancer. They demand that prospective patients make a one-hundred-thousand-euro deposit before the treatment even begins! That's the only thing the housekeeper seems to have gotten wrong—that clinic isn't just about pain management. They claim to have a sixty percent success rate, which is phenomenally higher than a patient at a normal hospital with cancer as advanced as his."

"Sixty percent?" I repeated, confused by her statement. After the will had been found, Simone had said the treatment would have extended his life, but would not have cured him. It was more about pain management, she'd said. So had Harold lied to her, in order to get his newly discovered daughter out of his life? Or had Simone lied to us?

"Why he didn't trust his wife with this news, but did tell his illegitimate daughter, is beyond me."

I wondered the same thing, but didn't want Tammy to know that. "Maybe it was easier for him to tell her, because they had no history together. He would have been less emotionally attached, you would think."

"I suppose, though it doesn't make it any easier. Nor does learning about Simone in this way make me want to welcome her into the family with open arms."

Tammy whipped her head up to lock eyes with me. "Did you know that right before the party started, my darling husband pulled me aside to share his great news with me—that he had another daughter all this time! I thought, alright, that's nice for him, to discover a by-product of a youthful adventure. It's not as if he actually loved Simone's mother. Heck, he couldn't even recall her name when I asked him about her. It was just some floozy housekeeper he had a fling with when he was a teenager visiting his family here at the house. I bet that's why he was no longer welcome here—his aunt didn't want the girl to get her claws in him. But that doesn't mean that he had to give her everything. We were the ones who stuck with him, through thick and thin. Doesn't that count for anything?"

Tammy begun to tear up, more at the thought of all that money he'd left to Simone, I suspected, when something she had just said gave me pause. "So this house was in his family's hands?"

"Yes, his father's sister lived here until her death. Jeeves had been her manservant and came with the house. When Harold was younger, the whole family would spend the summers here. But when he became a teenager, that all stopped. I suppose him getting that servant girl pregnant was to blame, although nobody told Harold about her condition."

Poor Simone. Harold's family had kept her mother's pregnancy from Harold. That explained why he had never contacted her again. I picked up one of the titles to the prayerbooks, noting the provenance information listed. It seemed complete. "So are you going to give this paperwork to Simone?"

"Are you daft?" Tammy snarled. "Why would I do anything to help that intruder? No, I want to have a talk with Wainwright's representative when he comes to collect the books, so I'm going to hang on to these. I know the sales agreement dictates that the money is deposited in that trust fund for her, but I believe we can find a workaround."

I paused to think of how Tammy could make the collector renege on the terms that he'd already agreed to. "Let me guess, you are going to offer him a significant discount if he deposits the money into your account, instead."

Tammy winked as she raised her glass to me. "I knew you were sharp. After all I did for Harold, I deserve the money far more than Simone does."

"And if you don't get your way…"

"Then I'll be broke until we can sell this villa. Do you want a drink? The bar's over there—you can choose your own poison."

I shook my head, declining her offer, as I tried to work up some sympathy for Tammy's predicament, but it was hard to do so when we were sitting in a multimillion-dollar home that was now officially hers. "Are you going to stay or go back to the States?"

"I'm stuck here until I can sell this monstrosity. That's going to be a challenge, in and of itself. This is all his cousins' fault. They couldn't afford to keep it running after their great-aunt died and nobody would pay the price they were asking for it. So after he retired, Mr. Chivalrous stepped in without even consulting me and bought this place."

"But he has other properties in America, doesn't he?"

"He used to, but he'd invested in a new toy company that lost far more money than it ever made. Unfortunately, it took him several years to get it through his thick skull that the company was never going to succeed. I don't know how much specifically, but he did have to sell our chalet in Aspen to cover his losses. And after he retired, he sold the beach house in Malibu and our apartment in San Francisco, where we were living before we moved over here, to pay for this villa. I didn't find out until the movers showed up to pack up our apartment."

My jaw dropped open. "So let me get this straight, Harold sold those properties and bought this house, before he informed you of his decisions? And you had no idea he was considering buying a house abroad?"

My mind was blown. My husband, Carlos, had sometimes made an executive decision for us as a couple, but those choices had more to do with which color bath towel would be best for the guest suite, never anything so significant as a new home.

"No, he did not. That's Harold for you. He was always changing his mind on a whim, with no consideration for how his decision would affect others."

"But why did he want to move to France?" I still couldn't get over the sudden change in location.

Tammy's laugh was bitter. "That's a great question. I thought it was because he wanted to travel around Europe with me, but that was not the case. I intentionally filled his office with travel memorabilia that I'd found in local shops to try to inspire him, but I don't think he noticed any of it."

She waved at a set of shelves hanging on the back wall. From where I was sitting, I could see a Nepalese prayer wheel, Balinese flying dragon, an Australian boomerang, and a vase made from Murano glass.

"Perhaps he thought living abroad would make us more sophisticated, somehow. Or maybe it was simply because it was something he hadn't done yet. Harold was always searching for a new challenge or experience to occupy him. You do see all sorts of shows featuring families giving the expat life a go and loving it. Yet as romantic as buying a house abroad and fixing it up sounds, it's really quite a bit of hard work. And once you're finished, you're stuck in the middle of nowhere."

She took a large swig of her mimosa before adding, "Not that Harold remained interested in the house for long. Once he'd possessed whatever he had set out to obtain, it seemed to lose its allure. That's why he was going to sell off part of his book collection, so he could reinvest the money in something else. Harold always has preferred new shiny things to the old faithful ones."

Was she talking about collectibles or people, I wondered. It sure felt more like the latter. Considering I was not in the mood to put on my psychiatrist's hat and help her work through her marital problems with her late husband, I ignored her last remark.

"Is that why you and Roger decided to kill him?"

Tammy sighed and looked away. "He had been acting distant for quite some time, but whenever I tried to talk to him about it, he would snap at me and retreat to his office. Then recently it became obvious that he and Simone were getting close. Things came to a head when he suddenly canceled the auction without giving me a valid reason. I thought he was going through some foolish midlife crisis and he was planning on running away with her, and taking his book collection with him, to fund their new life together. I never considered that she was his daugh—"

Tammy choked on the last word, unable to bring herself to say it aloud. Instead, she closed her eyes and inhaled deeply, before continuing. "I could sense something was changing and assumed the worst—that Harold was going to write me out of his will and then leave me. I just didn't know when. That's why I called Roger."

"So you did know that he had already changed his will to benefit Simone?" I asked, stunned by her confession.

"No! I had heard him talking to his lawyer about updating it, but I swear I did not know he had already drawn up a new one."

As I studied her flushed cheeks and tear-stained eyes, I couldn't help but believe her.

Tammy stood up and walked unsteadily to the mini-bar to pour herself another drink. "Do you know, when we first found Harold's body, I really did think Roger had pushed the bookcase over. I was glad that he hadn't killed his dad—it would have put him in therapy for life. Especially since we were too late; Harold had already changed his will to favor Simone."

Wow, it's incredible you didn't think about that earlier, I grumbled internally, knowing it was better to keep my sarcastic thoughts to myself. Instead, I said aloud, "So if Roger did not do it, who do you think did push the bookcase over?"

She picked up her drink and swirled the last few drops around the bottom, as she seemed to contemplate my query. "That's a good question. I would love it if Simone did it, but she really didn't have a reason to, did she? She's the one who inherits the most in Harold's new will, but she didn't know that he had already changed it—just like Roger and me," she emphasized, before continuing, "I suppose that leaves Billy."

Something about her comment niggled at my brain. I had one more fact to check before I found the Baroness and hashed everything out with her. "Speaking of your children, what is Roger going to do now? It sounds like he has quite a few financial problems."

Tammy smiled sadly as she stood up. "I'm not willing to talk about my child with a journalist. In fact, I probably shouldn't have told you anything. It's time to clean up this mess. Most of this paperwork can be tossed. I better get some garbage bags."

35

Chatting Up The Staff

When I pushed the kitchen door open, one staff member was washing up the cutlery from breakfast, while another was busy drying it. I wondered for a moment why they didn't use the dishwasher, until I realized the silverware must be actual silver.

Both women turned and smiled when I entered. "Are you looking for Simone?" the older of the two asked, in heavily accented English. "She just went up to her room."

"Oh, great, thanks. Actually, I wanted to ask you two something."

Something in my tone must have set her on edge, for the woman's friendly smile turned into a grimace. "Oh?"

"I'm not trying to get anyone into trouble. I was just curious if Harold had asked you to witness him signing any documents the night of the party." I shot her my biggest "you can trust me" grin, hoping to win her over.

The woman scowled at me. "What do you mean—you are just curious? You are a journalist, *non?*"

I sighed and let my shoulders slump. "You got me there. Look, I'm going to level with you. Tammy is running around saying that the will isn't valid because it wasn't witnessed by two people. But that notary, Jacques, has been telling everyone that it is valid because two female staff members witnessed Harold's signature. I assumed he meant you two. I just wanted to hear—from the source—which story was true."

The woman threw down her dish towel. "Why does that woman lie so? What does it matter—I already told the police and Mr. Moreau is dead, so he cannot be angry with me."

"Mr. Moreau?" I mumbled softly, before realizing she meant Harold.

"Yes, Mr. Moreau, my employer. He asked us to watch him sign some documents so his notary could notarize them."

"And which documents were those?"

She sucked up her breath before blurting out, "Mr. Moreau's new will and a sales contract with a man named Wainwright. Mr. Moreau paid us extra to be his witnesses, but don't tell his notary that. It was illegal for him to do so, but quite kind."

"Did Tammy know that you two had witnessed Harold signing his new will? Could she have been standing outside the room when the documents were notarized?" I asked, certain Tammy had been lurking by the door.

"No, Mr. Moreau did not want his wife to know about the new documents. He even checked the hall to make certain she was not there," the housekeeper stammered and blushed. "You will not tell Mrs. Moreau, *non?*"

"*Non*, I mean, no. This will definitely stay between us. I was also curious, did you tell Simone that she was the main beneficiary of Harold's new will?"

The woman cocked her head and gazed at me as if I was the one who was confused. "How would I know what he had left to whom? Mr. Moreau did ask us to witness his signature, but we were not allowed to read through the documents."

So much for that theory, I thought. "Alright. Well, I guess that's everything. Thanks for helping me understand this horrible situation better. I'll get out of your hair."

The woman began to turn back to her kitchen duties until I added, "There's just one last thing—did you notice if anyone was standing in the hallway when you left the office?"

She frowned. "No, only Simone. She brought lunch for Mr. Moreau and his guest after we finished signing everything. The papers were still on the desk when she came in, so I suppose she could have seen them."

"Oh." Her words took my breath away. I hadn't expected her to name

Simone. "Alright. Thanks for your help."

"De rien." It is nothing, she answered, as her relief shone through her smile.

I smiled back, but inside my stomach was churning. If Simone saw the freshly signed will on Harold's desk, she could have assumed that he had changed it to benefit her, as he had repeatedly promised. Which gave her thirty million reasons to get rid of Harold.

Instead of feeling elation that I was closing in on the killer, all I felt was sick. All the arrows pointed towards Simone, but I couldn't bring myself to accuse her of this heinous crime. There had to be another explanation. She was so grateful to have finally found her biological father—she couldn't have murdered him, could she?

36

A Flash of Insight

I stood outside the kitchen door, frozen in place, uncertain what to do next. Although I knew I should call Detective Nobel and tell him what the kitchen staff had told me, it felt like throwing Simone under the bus. If she was not the killer, I would never forgive myself for putting her through being a suspect in her own father's murder investigation. Before I called anyone, I had to talk to her myself and hear what she had to say.

A peal of laughter made me turn to the living room as a flash from one of the guests' cameras went off. Its burst of light brought with it a burst of insight.

What if my camera had captured a picture of the killer just before it was crushed? If, by some miracle, I had photographic evidence, I wouldn't have to interrogate anyone else. It was a long shot for sure, but desperate times called for desperate measures.

With a spring in my step, I changed direction, heading back to the library. My bobby pin was already in hand, ready for lock-picking duties, when I noticed that there was no need. The door was slightly ajar, and a light was on at the back of the space.

I gently pushed the door open, wondering who I would find inside. It was Simone, sitting in a chair with one of Harold's illuminated manuscripts in her lap. I sucked in my breath, frustrated that the universe would not let me delay this conversation any longer.

The art historian in me shuddered at the sight of Simone licking her fingertips before turning one of the fragile pages. Her bacteria-filled saliva was not good for the vellum.

Simone's head whipped around at the sound of my heels on the tile, her expression a mix of dread and irritation. At least, until she registered who it was. "Hi, Carmen. It's good to see a friendly face."

I nodded at the book in her lap as I pushed a stray hair behind my ear. "They are beautiful, aren't they?"

"They really are. It's almost too bad Papa already sold them. I somehow feel closer to him, sitting here, looking at these images."

I took in the vibrant blues and reds that brought Mary and baby Jesus to life in the intricate illustration depicting a moment in their holy lives. "Is that the Lindeman Book of Hours?"

She smiled up at me, and something about the tilt of her chin made me think of her father. "It is—you really know your prayer books! Harold told me this was one of his favorites."

When she ran her hand over the illustration, allowing her wet fingers to linger on the page and paints, it took all of my willpower not to rip her arm away from the delicate sheet. Yet based on her rapt expression, she seemed to have forgotten that I was there, and had already retreated into the book in her hand as she continued slowly turning the pages and absorbing the illustrations.

The longer I stood there, the more uncomfortable I felt for interrupting her private time. I knew how difficult it was to grow up without a father, and I didn't know how I would react if I'd suddenly met him, only to lose him again. It would feel as if he'd died twice, I bet.

Right now, the last thing I wanted to do was have to interrogate her, not while she was trying to have a peaceful moment with her father's memories.

When I turned to leave, my movement roused her out of her meditative trance. "What can I do for you?"

"Oh, gosh, it's not important. I had my camera with me that, um, night and figure it's here under the books somewhere. There are several photos of the Baroness that my magazine wants to use—if the memory card even survived the crash, that is. I can come back later to look for it. I'm sorry to have disturbed you."

I was already backing out of the space when Simone closed the prayer book more forcefully than I liked, then rose. "You're not intruding. After all, you have been so kind to me, the least I can do is help you look. It's one of those old-fashioned SLR cameras, right? I saw you taking pictures at the party with it. My mom used to have one of those."

Before I could reassure her that it was not important in the slightest, Simone added, "I thought I saw it on the table between the two chairs…"

When she rose and walked to the exact spot I'd left it, moments before the bookcase came crashing down, my jaw went slack.

All I could do was watch as she dug through the numerous books still stacked up on the floor, until she'd hit paydirt, several minutes later. My crushed camera in hand, she turned and smiled triumphantly. *"Et voilà!"*

When I saw my camera, my mind froze, momentarily unable to accept the truth, as did my body. So Simone rose and walked it over to me. "Yikes, there isn't much left. I hope your magazine's tech guys can salvage the memory card."

She stretched her arm out, the crushed digital SLR camera body in her hand. The lens had snapped off, I noted. Not that it mattered anymore.

Simone looked so triumphant, it was clear that she had not yet realized her mistake.

I stared at her, trying to understand how she could have done something so evil. "Harold left you everything. Why did you have to kill him?"

"What do you mean?" Her sweet smile cracked slightly as she blinked her lashes at me, feigning naiveté.

I was such a sucker to have believed in her innocence for so long.

"The only way you could have known where I'd left my camera was if you had been in the library with me and Harold. I only set it down there for a moment, just before the bookcase fell over. Which means you must have pushed it."

As Simone looked to the smashed-up camera in her hand, her face drained of color as awareness appeared to dawn on her. "This?" she asked, her voice suddenly as thick and slow as molasses. "No, I, um, saw something shiny under the books earlier, that's all. It was sheer luck that I found it so fast."

"Come on, Simone, stop lying! Admit it—you pushed the bookcase onto Harold!"

My voice rose an octave as the realization that I was standing across from a potentially sociopathic killer sunk in. If Harold really was her long-lost father, killing him was a funny way of showing that she wanted to get to know him better.

Simone's eyes narrowed as she threw the camera at me, causing me to jerk to one side, leaving her a free path to run past me.

"Help! Simone killed Harold—don't let her get away!" I screamed at the top of my lungs as I turned to follow.

Luckily, everyone on the first floor seemed to have heard me. Before I could reach the library door, Jacques and Gary had their hands on Simone's arms. Tammy stood before her and was pulling her hand back to slap the young woman, when I rushed forward. "No, stop! The police are going to arrest her—there's no need for violence."

"She killed my husband!" Tammy screamed, tears streaming down her cheeks.

"Yeah, meaning she beat you and Roger to it. Come on, Tammy, no one believes you're sorry he's gone."

Tammy's hand flew to her temple, just before she fainted, her body dropping heavily to the floor.

As the guests rushed over to help, Simone saw her chance to go free and made another break for it. She was almost at the front door, when an umbrella shot out and tripped her.

"Ow!"

Simone went down hard. Moments later, the butler stood over her, gazing down at the former housekeeper with loathing in his eyes.

"How dare you accuse me of theft. In my fifty-five years of service, I have never stolen from my employers or their guests. It's simply unbecoming for a person in my position to do so."

Having said his piece, Jeeves turned and walked upstairs, towards the kitchen.

37

Killer In Our Midst

Simone sat on the edge of her chair, surrounded by a ring of guests, as we waited in the living room for the police to return.

Tammy, now fully conscious, stared at her as if Simone was an unsolvable puzzle she just had to crack. "I don't understand why you did it—he left you everything."

"Sure, but for how long? He could have changed his mind again, or you could have persuaded him to tear up the new will. Or worse—he could have recovered and lived another ten years. He was going to Switzerland for medical treatment, and that clinic has an impressive success rate. Where would that leave me? The sale was contingent on his death—I wouldn't see a dime until then."

"But he was your dad. I thought you couldn't wait to get to know him better," I whispered, angry that I had let myself be so easily misled. She had manipulated me like a pro—I would have done anything to protect her. But, in fact, she was the killer all along.

Simone's laugh bordered on manic. "He was no father to me! I hated him for destroying my mother. I never knew the sparkling young thing she supposedly was, before Harold got his hands on her. Maman truly believed that Harold would take care of us, but he never even tried to get in touch with her after he flew back to America! Her pining away for him destroyed my childhood and any chance of her finding happiness elsewhere. I wanted to ruin his life, like he did mine."

Simone looked so forlorn, I wanted to reach out and hug her, until I remembered what she really was—a liar and murderer. Instead, I asked, "Is that why you took this job—so you could kill him?"

"It wasn't my original intention, but I did want to make him pay. He owed me for all those years of heartache. I figured I could steal enough jewelry and silverware to fund a new life somewhere else. But once I got here, I realized there were better ways to hurt Harold."

"But he wrote you into his will! He must not have been as horrible as you're making him out to be," I retorted.

"Only because he felt guilty about how things turned out. He didn't even remember my mother's name!" she howled, as tears streamed down her face. "Harold did tear up after I told him about her, and said he was grateful to finally know why he was never welcome at Villa Saint Marie again. He thought he'd offended his aunt in some way, but in reality his family wanted to keep him away from my mother. But he cared more about his lost youth than Maman or me!"

Simone tilted her chin up. "That's why I kept the guilt trip up, until he offered to make things right by including me in his will. When he told me he'd decided to leave his book collection to me, Harold unwittingly gave me the ideal way to exact my revenge, and live the life I should have been living, but was denied by his snobbish family. It was perfect."

"Perfect?" I was stunned by her calm demeanor. She didn't care about Harold one bit. What a fool I was to have believed her.

Simone bit her lower lip and looked away. "Well, almost perfect. The only catch was I wouldn't inherit anything until he died. So he had to go; I just had to wait for the right moment. When I brought lunch to his office and saw the notarized will on his desk, I knew I had to act fast. But there were so many guests going in and out of the library, I began to think my plan wasn't going to work. Until he went in to talk to you and asked that you not be disturbed."

She sat back in the chair and crossed one leg over the other, as if she was chatting with a good friend. The room was so quiet, I could hear my heart beat.

"How did you know that Tammy had removed the bolts?" I finally asked, my voice a whisper.

"I didn't. The bookcase seemed like a fitting murder weapon, though. It took a little effort to get it going, but once the bookcase got moving, gravity took over. I guess I have Tammy to thank for that."

We all looked to Harold's wife, who turned her gaze down towards her lap.

"You had a shot at happiness!" I shouted, my latent frustration boiling over. I'd never had that chance. Simone had the opportunity to get to know her biological father, but chose revenge instead. And for what? She would never be able to spend any of his cash, but instead would pay for her crimes with several years of her freedom.

All I could do was shake my head to stop myself from crying, heartbroken that money had triumphed over love.

38

Justice Served

An hour later, Detective Nobel was back at Villa Saint Marie and in a much better mood than his previous visits. My having pinpointed the killer for him probably had something to do with it.

Watching the police officers take Simone away in handcuffs sent a thrill of pride through my veins. It always felt good to see justice served. The fact that my husband's killer had never been found bothered me deeply. I couldn't find closure, no matter how hard I tried.

Wrapping up a case conjured up a feeling of satisfaction like no other, one I missed tremendously. I hadn't been certain that working in the field again was a smart move, not after what happened to Carlos. But now, standing on the cusp of a mission accomplished, it felt great to be back. I only hoped my employer agreed.

But first, I had to play nice with the local cops.

After thanking the guests for their cooperation and announcing that we were all free to go, the detective called out my name and waved me over.

"So I have you to thank for this arrest," he said in his charmingly thick French accent. "I must apologize for my rude behavior last time we spoke. I had not slept in two days because of the storm and my nerves were frayed. After a good night's sleep and talk with your boss, I understand you had nothing to do with this crime, and that you were not planning on stealing the Avron prayer book, but intended to bring it to the proper authorities."

"Thank you." My voice cracked as I struggled with my emotions. It sounded like I was going to be able to leave this villa with my cover still intact. "Am I also free to go?"

His glowing smile set my mind at ease. He rummaged through his jacket until he pulled out a small blue book.

"Here, this is yours."

I grabbed my passport and held it to my chest, feeling relief flowing through my veins.

"Before you go, can you tell me more about your next objective?"

"No, but I promise to alert the proper authorities if I find another stolen object, instead of taking it with me."

"I mean, is your next assignment in France?" he pushed.

"No, I am on my way to Belgium."

The relief on his face was evident. "I hope the rest of your stay in Europe is trouble-free."

"Me, too," I chuckled.

He bowed and let me pass.

I rushed upstairs to collect the Baroness and our suitcases. She greeted me with a hearty hug. "Your first assignment back is a success! How does it feel?"

"It feels great!"

"I am so proud of you, Carmen. I knew you were the right choice for this assignment. It's good to see you feeling like your old self and that, after what happened to Carlos, you're not afraid."

Her sharp insight struck like a knife. I swallowed a tear, glad to have the Baroness back in my life. She was a good person deep down, despite her bling-bling exterior.

"So, what's next?" I asked, keeping my tone as light as possible.

"Before we head to Belgium, Reggie wants us to stop off in Calais. A collector may have a sketch by Henri Matisse that was stolen from a castle outside of London two years ago. It's one of twenty sketches still in existence, so you'll have to get a look at the back to verify it. The collector is having a party to celebrate his eightieth birthday tomorrow night, and we're on the guest list. Reggie just sent over the invitation and dossier."

My mind began spinning, thinking of the reasons I'd used in the past to convince an owner to remove a sketch from its frame. Flattery would definitely play a part. In my experience, it was better to use honey than a stick. At least, initially.

A few minutes later, after having double-checked the contents of her bag, my partner locked her suitcase and straightened her tiara. "I am ready to leave."

"Fantastic. I hope the car is drivable. I really want to get out of here."

We gathered up our things and headed downstairs, keeping the goodbyes to a minimum. Most of the other guests were also rushing to leave, with Jacques leading the pack. So far, he seemed to have been overlooked by the authorities. Despite his possible shortcomings, he seemed like a nice guy and I rather hoped he would get away with whatever it was he was doing.

Countess Ursula, to my partner's chagrin, was the most enthusiastic. "See you in Belgium," she purred from the driver's seat of her MG Roadster.

I raised an eyebrow at my partner as Ursula sped off.

"She's rented an apartment in Paris until August and is doing the same circuit we are."

"Oh, joy."

"Exactly. She's the one the person I would rather not see again," the Baroness groused.

As we walked out to our rental, I had to watch my step for fear of tripping over a fallen branch and breaking a leg. *That's all I need is to get injured again*, I thought. After a three-year hiatus, I had successfully completed my first assignment. I preferred not to add a trip to the hospital to today's agenda.

Once we were safely buckled up and ready to roll, a surge of joy rose from within, filling me with an immense rush of pride that I hadn't felt in three years.

With a smile on my face, I put the keys in the ignition and looked to my partner. "Ready for our next adventure?"

"I am," she said after adjusting her tiara and seatbelt once more. "While you're driving, I'll read you what Reggie sent over about the Matisse. Here's the address."

"Fantastic, that'll give me a chance to prepare." I ticked our destination, a spa-hotel located outside of Calais, into the rental's satnav before revving the engine, our car spewing gravel as we shot down the driveway. It felt good to be leaving this place behind. With a little luck, the rest of our assignments would go more smoothly.

When we turned left at the end of Harold's driveway, I waved goodbye to Villa Saint Marie, then pushed the gas pedal to the floor and tore down the provincial highway. For the first time in years, I felt unstoppable. In two days' time, I had verified a stolen book, arranged for its return, and solved a murder. I'd say I was doing pretty well for someone just coming out of retirement. Now I was off on another quest, with Myrtle to do my bidding and my favorite partner by my side.

What could possibly go wrong?

Thanks for reading *Collecting Can Be Murder*!

Reviews really do help readers decide whether they want to take a chance on a new author. If you enjoyed this story, please consider posting a review on BookBub, on Goodreads, or with your favorite retailer. I appreciate it!
Jennifer S. Alderson

I hope you will join Carmen De Luca for her next adventure in *A Statue To Die For*.
After a movie prop is used to murder a washed-up Hollywood film director, art sleuth Carmen De Luca has to flush out the killer before she becomes the next victim…

Acknowledgements

The idea for this new mystery series came to me after I was invited to write a short story for an eBook anthology collection entitled *A Bookworm of a Suspect*. The resulting story, *A Book To Die For*, inspired the characters and plotlines for the Carmen De Luca Art Sleuth Mysteries.

However, this is not the first time Carmen and Rhonda have made an appearance in my work. The two art-loving friends were part of Lana Hansen's tour group in my cozy mystery *Death by Gondola* and helped her solve the case! Although the pair's backgrounds have changed somewhat since then, their friendship as introduced in that cozy mystery form the heart of this new series.

My wonderful family deserves a huge thanks for helping me create time to write, as well as for encouraging me to keep developing new characters and series. I am so grateful for their love and support.

I am also indebted to my editor, Sadye Scott-Hainchek of The Fussy Librarian, for her outstanding work and advice.

The cover designer for this series and my Travel Can Be Murder Cozy Mysteries, Elizabeth Mackey, continues to amaze me with her gorgeous and fun designs.

Thanks go to you too, dear reader, for taking a chance on a new series. I look forward to sharing more of Carmen De Luca's adventures with you quite soon.

Until then, happy reading and travels!

About the Author

Jennifer S. Alderson was born in San Francisco, grew up in Seattle, and currently lives in Amsterdam. After traveling extensively around Asia, Oceania, and Central America, she lived in Darwin, Australia, before settling in the Netherlands.

Jennifer's love of travel, art, and culture inspires her award-winning Zelda Richardson Mystery series, her Travel Can Be Murder Cozy Mysteries, and her Carmen De Luca Art Sleuth Mysteries. Her background in journalism, multimedia development, and art history enriches her novels.

When not writing, she can be found perusing a museum, biking around Amsterdam, or enjoying a coffee along the canal while planning her next research trip.

Visit Jennifer's website [www.jennifersalderson.com] to learn more about her books and sign up for her mailing list.

Books by Jennifer S. Alderson:

Carmen De Luca Art Sleuth Mysteries
Collecting Can Be Murder
A Statue To Die For
Forgeries and Fatalities
A Killer Inheritance

Travel Can Be Murder Cozy Mysteries
Death on the Danube: A New Year's Murder in Budapest
Death by Baguette: A Valentine's Day Murder in Paris

Death by Windmill: A Mother's Day Murder in Amsterdam
Death by Bagpipes: A Summer Murder in Edinburgh
Death by Fountain: A Christmas Murder in Rome
Death by Leprechaun: A Saint Patrick's Day Murder in Dublin
Death by Flamenco: An Easter Murder in Seville
Death by Gondola: A Springtime Murder in Venice
Death by Puffin: A Bachelorette Party Murder in Reykjavik

Zelda Richardson Art Mysteries
The Lover's Portrait: An Art Mystery
Rituals of the Dead: An Artifact Mystery
Marked for Revenge: An Art Heist Thriller
The Vermeer Deception: An Art Mystery

Standalone Travel Thriller
Down and Out in Kathmandu: A Backpacker Mystery

Death on the Danube: A New Year's Murder in Budapest

Book One of the Travel Can Be Murder Cozy Mystery Series

Who knew a New Year's trip to Budapest could be so deadly? The tour must go on—even with a killer in their midst...

Recent divorcee Lana Hansen needs a break. Her luck has run sour for going on a decade, ever since she got fired from her favorite job as an investigative reporter. When her fresh start in Seattle doesn't work out as planned, Lana ends up unemployed and penniless on Christmas Eve.

Dotty Thompson, her landlord and the owner of Wanderlust Tours, is also in a tight spot after one of her tour guides ends up in the hospital, leaving her a guide short on Christmas Day.

When Dotty offers her a job leading the tour group through Budapest, Hungary, Lana jumps at the chance. It's the perfect way to ring in the new year and pay her rent!

What starts off as the adventure of a lifetime quickly turns into a nightmare when Carl, her fellow tour guide, is found floating in the Danube River. Was it murder or accidental death? Suspects abound when Lana discovers almost everyone on the tour had a bone to pick with Carl.

But Dotty insists the tour must go on, so Lana finds herself trapped with nine murder suspects. When another guest turns up dead, Lana has to figure out who the killer is before she too ends up floating in the Danube.

Excerpt from *Death on the Danube*
Chapter One: A Trip to Budapest

"You want me to go where, Dotty? And do what?" Lana Hansen had trouble keeping the incredulity out of her voice. She was thrilled, as always, by her landlord's unwavering support and encouragement. But now Lana was beginning to wonder whether Dotty Thompson was becoming mentally unhinged.

"To escort a tour group in Budapest, Hungary. It'll be easy enough for a woman of your many talents."

Lana snorted with laughter. *Ha! What talents?* she thought. Her resume was indeed long: disgraced investigative journalist, injured magician's assistant, former kayaking guide, and now part-time yoga instructor—emphasis on "part-time."

"You'll get to celebrate New Year's while earning a paycheck and enjoying a free trip abroad, to boot. You've been moaning for months about wanting a fresh start. Well, this is as fresh as it gets!" Dotty exclaimed, causing her Christmas-bell earrings to jangle. She was wrapped up in a rainbow-colored bathrobe, a hairnet covering the curlers she set every morning. They were standing inside her living room, Lana still wearing her woolen navy jacket and rain boots. Behind Dotty's ample frame, Lana could see the many decorations and streamers she'd helped to hang up for the Christmas bash last night. Lana was certain that if Dotty's dogs hadn't woken her up, her landlord would have slept the day away.

"Working as one of your tour guides wasn't exactly what I had in mind, Dotty."

"I wouldn't ask you if I had any other choice." Dotty's tone switched from flippant to pleading. "Yesterday one of the guides and two guests crashed into each other while skibobbing outside of Prague, and all are hospitalized. Thank goodness none are in critical condition. But the rest of the group is leaving for Budapest in the morning, and Carl can't do it on his own. He's just not client-friendly enough to pull it off. And I need those five-star reviews, Lana."

Dotty was not only a property manager, she was also the owner of several successful small businesses. Lana knew Wanderlust Tours was Dotty's favorite and that she would do anything to ensure its continued success. Lana also knew that the tour company was suffering from the increased competition from online booking sites and was having trouble building its audience and generating traffic to its social media accounts. But asking Lana to fill in as a guide seemed desperate, even for Dotty, and even if it was the day after Christmas. Lana shook her head slowly. "I don't know. I'm not qualified to—"

Dotty grabbed one of Lana's hands and squeezed. "Qualified, shmalified. I didn't have any tour guide credentials when I started this company fifteen years ago, and that hasn't made a bit of difference. You enjoy leading those kayaking tours, right? This is the same thing, but for a while longer."

The older lady glanced down at the plastic cards in her other hand, shaking her head. "Besides, you know I love you like a daughter, but I can't accept these gift cards in lieu of rent. If you do this for me, you don't have to pay me back for the past two months' rent. I am offering you the chance of a lifetime. What have you got to lose?"

If you are enjoying the book, why not pick up your copy now and keep reading? Available as paperback, large print edition, eBook, and in Kindle Unlimited.

The Lover's Portrait: An Art Mystery

Book One in the Zelda Richardson Art Mystery Series

"*The Lover's Portrait* is a well-written mystery with engaging characters and a lot of heart. The perfect novel for those who love art and mysteries!" – Reader's Favorite, 5-star medal

"Well worth reading for what the main character discovers—not just about the portrait mentioned in the title, but also the sobering dangers of Amsterdam during World War II." – IndieReader

A portrait holds the key to recovering a cache of looted artwork, secreted away during World War II, in this captivating historical art thriller set in the 1940s and present-day Amsterdam.

When a Dutch art dealer hides the stock from his gallery – rather than turn it over to his Nazi blackmailer – he pays with his life, leaving a treasure trove of modern masterpieces buried somewhere in Amsterdam, presumably lost forever. That is, until American art history student Zelda Richardson sticks her nose in.

After studying for a year in the Netherlands, Zelda scores an internship at the prestigious Amsterdam Historical Museum, where she works on an exhibition of paintings and sculptures once stolen by the Nazis, lying unclaimed in Dutch museum depots almost seventy years later. When two women claim the same painting, the portrait of a young girl entitled *Irises*, Zelda is tasked with investigating the painting's history and soon finds evidence that one of the two women must be lying about her past. Before she can figure out which one it is and why, Zelda learns about the Dutch art dealer's concealed collection. And that *Irises* is the key to finding it all.

Her discoveries make her a target of someone willing to steal – and even kill – to find the missing paintings. As the list of suspects grows, Zelda realizes she has to track down the lost collection and unmask a killer if she wants to survive.

Excerpt from *The Lover's Portrait*
Chapter 1: Two More Crates

June 26, 1942

Just two more crates, then our work is finally done, Arjan reminded himself as he bent down to grasp the thick twine handles, his back muscles already yelping in protest. Drops of sweat were burning his eyes, blurring his vision. "You can do this," he said softly, heaving the heavy oak box upwards with an audible grunt.

Philip nodded once, then did the same. Together they lugged their loads across the moonlit room, down the metal stairs, and into the cool subterranean space below. After hoisting the last two crates onto a stack close to the ladder, Arjan smiled in satisfaction, slapping Philip on the back as he regarded their work. One hundred and fifty-two crates holding his most treasured objects, and those of so many of his friends, were finally safe. Relief briefly overcame the panic and dread he'd been feeling for longer than he could remember. Preparing the space and artwork had taken more time than he'd hoped it would, but they'd done it. Now he could leave Amsterdam knowing he'd stayed true to his word. Arjan glanced over at Philip, glad he'd trusted him. He stretched out a hand towards the older man. "They fit perfectly."

Philip answered with a hasty handshake and a tight smile before nodding towards the ladder. "Shall we?"

He is right, Arjan thought, *there is still so much to do*. They climbed back up into the small shed and closed the heavy metal lid, careful to cushion its fall.

They didn't want to give the neighbors an excuse to call the Gestapo. Not when they were so close to being finished.

Philip picked up a shovel and scooped sand onto the floor, letting Arjan rake it out evenly before adding more. When the sand was an inch deep, they shifted the first layer of heavy cement tiles into place, careful to fit them snug up against each other.

As they heaved and pushed, Arjan allowed himself to think about the future for the first time in weeks. Hiding the artwork was only the first step; he still had a long way to go before he could stop looking over his shoulder. First, back to his place to collect their suitcases. Then, a short walk to Central Station where second-class train tickets to Venlo were waiting. Finally, a taxi ride to the Belgian border where his contact would provide him with falsified travel documents and a chauffeur-driven Mercedes-Benz. The five Rembrandt etchings in his suitcase would guarantee safe passage to Switzerland. From Geneva he should be able to make his way through the demilitarized zone to Lyon, then down to Marseilles. All he had to do was keep a few steps ahead of Oswald Drechsler.

Just thinking about the hawk-nosed Nazi made him work faster. So far he'd been able to clear out his house and storage spaces without Drechsler noticing. Their last load, the canvases stowed in his gallery, was the riskiest, but he'd had no choice. His friends trusted him—no, counted on him—to keep their treasures safe. He couldn't let them down now. Not after all he'd done wrong.

If you are enjoying the story so far, why not pick up your copy now and keep reading? Available as eBook, audiobook, and paperback.

CPSIA information can be obtained
at www.ICGtesting.com
Printed in the USA
LVHW041645020723
751369LV00005B/294